THE CROSSROADS

For more than forty years,
Yearling has been the leading name
in classic and award-winning literature
for young readers.

Yearling books feature children's
favorite authors and characters,
providing dynamic stories of adventure,
humor, history, mystery, and fantasy.

Trust Yearling paperbacks to entertain,
inspire, and promote the love of reading
in all children.

OTHER YEARLING BOOKS YOU WILL ENJOY

CHRIS GRABENSTEIN

THE CROSSROADS

A YEARLING BOOK

This is a work of fiction. Names, characters, places, and incidents either are the product of the author's imagination or are used fictitiously. Any resemblance to actual persons, living or dead, events, or locales is entirely coincidental.

Copyright © 2008 by Chris Grabenstein

All rights reserved. Published in the United States by Yearling, an imprint of Random House Children's Books, a division of Random House, Inc., New York. Originally published in hardcover by Random House Books for Young Readers, in 2008.

Yearling and the jumping horse design are registered trademarks of Random House, Inc.

Visit us on the Web! www.randomhouse.com/kids

Educators and librarians, for a variety of teaching tools, visit us at www.randomhouse.com/teachers

Library of Congress Cataloging-in-Publication Data
Grabenstein, Chris.
The crossroads / Chris Grabenstein.
p. cm.
Summary: When eleven-year-old Zack Jennings moves to Connecticut with his father and new stepmother, they must deal with the ghosts left behind by a terrible accident, as well as another kind of ghost from Zack's past.
ISBN 978-0-375-84697-7 (trade) — ISBN 978-0-375-94697-4 (lib. bdg.) —
ISBN 978-0-375-84698-4 (pbk.)
[1. Ghosts—Fiction. 2. Stepmothers—Fiction. 3. Guilt—Fiction. 4. Traffic accidents—Fiction. 5. Moving, Household—Fiction. 6. Family life—Connecticut—Fiction.
7. Connecticut—Fiction.] I. Title.
PZ7.G7487Cro 2008 [Fic]—dc22 2007024803

Printed in the United States of America

10 9 8 7 6 5 4 3

First Yearling Edition

for Meghan, Sam & Rachel

Prologue

Have you ever seen a face hidden in the bark of a tree and known that the man trapped inside wanted to hurt you?

That's what Zack Jennings had always wanted to ask his father, but he never did, because he was afraid his dad would think he was just letting his imagination run wild again.

Except this time Zack was pretty certain he had seen a man's face hidden inside this huge gnarly tree over in the small park ringing the American Museum of Natural History.

Other kids might've seen lumpy bumps and knotholes. Zack saw angry eyes and a snarling mouth.

But Zack never did ask his father. Instead, he asked Mrs. Donna Schlampp, the librarian at his school, if she thought reincarnation extended to plants as well as animals. Could people come back as a tree or just as cows or some kind of bug? Mrs. Schlampp (who had a graduate degree in comparative theology but never got to use it except at dinner parties) said that, yes, some religions believed tormented souls could become trapped inside the elements of nature—most especially trees.

So according to one adult who'd been to college, the oak in the park could, indeed, have an anguished soul trapped beneath its bark.

Thanks a bunch, Mrs. Schlampp.

Fortunately, Zack and his dad were leaving New York City pretty soon. They were moving up to Connecticut right after his dad got married again.

That tree in the park? It wasn't coming with them.

But maybe Mrs. Schlampp could go visit it from time to time.

1

Billy O'Claire was doggy-dog tired.

He'd been trying to fix the toilet in the brand-new house for over six hours and the weather outside was extremely hot and muggy, especially for the Friday before Memorial Day.

Billy was sweating up a storm. Since nobody lived in the new house yet, they hadn't turned on the air-conditioning. His work shirt was a soppy sheet of wet cotton with full-moon stains oozing down below both armpits.

It was nine p.m.

He tightened one last nut, then gave the trip handle on the toilet a flick. Instead of the customary *whoosh* of water swirling into the bowl, Billy heard a roaring gur-gle. The toilet was working backward. He raised the lid and saw a commode burping up chunks of brown gunk. Leaves. Dirt. Twigs.

Nothing else, thank heaven, because nobody had actually *used* the toilet yet. This woodsy debris had to be seeping in from a cracked sewer line, and Billy realized they might have to rip up the newly sodded lawn to fix a drainpipe ruptured, most likely, by tree roots.

But that was a Monday-morning kind of problem.

Fortunately, it was Friday night and Billy was finished working for the week. He cranked the shutoff valve behind the toilet and went out to the driveway, where he had parked his pickup, the one with O'Claire's Plumbing painted on the door over where it used to say O'Claire's Painting and, before that, O'Claire's Satellite Television Repair.

Billy sat in the cab and drank half a gallon of water out of a glugging plastic jug and aimed two of the truck's air-conditioning vents up at his armpits.

It felt good. Real good.

He yawned and thought about grabbing a quick nap. Instead, he slammed the transmission into reverse and backed out of the driveway, not realizing that something wicked was lurking a little ways down the road—just waiting for the next doggy-dog-tired driver to come along.

A flashing red stoplight hung suspended over the intersection where County Route 13 crossed Connecticut State Highway 31.

A gigantic oak tree stood near one corner, and its

highest branch—as thick around as the trunk of any ordinary tree—suddenly started to move. No wind was blowing. No sports car zooming past had sent up a swirling wake. But the massive limb began to bend and rotate. It sensed an easy target approaching and, longing for a little fun, tore against itself—slowly at first, then with gathering speed. When the final strands ripped free, the bough broke off and fell like a two-ton truck, tearing down the blinking beacon.

Then the tree stopped moving.

Billy O'Claire remembered that there used to be a flashing red stoplight hanging over the intersection of 13 and 31. Tonight, however, there wasn't one.

Good.

Billy didn't want to stop. He needed to find a bathroom. Bad. Chugging half a gallon of water straight from the jug will do that to you. And he preferred a bathroom where the toilet didn't gurgle back at him. He pressed down on the gas pedal.

"*How dry I am,*" he crooned off-key. "*How wet I'll be, if I don't find . . .*"

Suddenly he saw someone standing in the middle of the road.

A cop.

A motorcycle cop—holding up his hand and commanding Billy to stop.

So Billy slammed on his brakes and the pickup skidded sideways. Tires screeched, the truck swerved, and he almost hooked on to the bumper of a car he hadn't even seen coming. He spun around and wound up on the far side of the intersection—backward and straddling a ditch.

Billy wasn't injured, just totally dazed. He could see the taillights of the car he had nearly hit as it zoomed up the highway. Glancing at his rearview mirror, he saw the cop standing next to his motorbike, which was very weird-looking—it had a moonfaced headlight and chrome fenders swooping up over its tires.

It's from the 1950s, Billy thought. *An old Harley Softail.* Billy liked old motorcycles. Wished he had one right now so he could hightail it out of there before the cop came over and started hassling him. Then Billy realized: The cop's uniform and hat looked old-fashioned, too.

It looks like he's from some black-and-white movie. One of those old monster movies where the police try to capture Godzilla.

The cop marched slowly toward the truck. Billy strained to see if it was anybody he knew, thinking this was some kind of practical joke. He tried to see the cop's face.

Only the cop didn't have one.

He had a crew cut and mirrored sunglasses and ears but no face!

Billy jerked up on his door handle hard. When it

wouldn't budge, he kicked the door open. He screamed once and scrambled out of the truck and ran as fast as he could up the highway.

The police officer didn't care about Billy O'Claire. Didn't chase after him.

His job was done for the night. He had prevented a horrible, possibly fatal, collision.

Something he had tried to do once before.

June 21, 1958.

The day he had died.

2

On the morning of his father's second wedding, Zack Jennings stood in a tuxedo on the mound of Shea Stadium, the first eleven-year-old to ever pitch for the New York Mets.

There were moving boxes set up in a diamond around the empty living room. Blankets and Pillows was first base. Kitchen Stuff was second. Books, third. A heavy cardboard china box was home plate because it had dishes in it. Dishes and *plates*.

Zack checked the signals from the catcher, shook his head. No way was he throwing a slider. Not with two outs in the bottom of the ninth, a full count, and imaginary men on first, second, and third. The bases were loaded.

"It all comes down to this one pitch," Zack said, narrating the scene. "He looks to the dugout." Zack glanced over at the stuffed animals lined up along the baseboard.

He looked to his coach and the grizzled bear gave him the signal: *Throw whatever you think is best, kid.*

Zack nodded. He understood. The old ball coach was giving him the game. It was Zack's to win or lose.

He pushed his eyeglasses up his nose. Some players laughed at any pitcher who wore his spectacles out on the mound. That is, they laughed until they saw Zack hurl his famous firebomb fandango fastball. Then they realized that the glasses were what gave Zack Jennings his supersonic vision, enabling him to place pitches precisely over that portion of the plate where no batter could possibly hit them.

Zack squeezed the spongy ball in his right fist. He glanced toward third, making sure the imaginary man wasn't taking too much of a lead. He raised his left leg.

"Here's the windup and the pitch. He's going with the fastball!"

Zack shifted into super-slo-mo and added sound effects: the *zoom* of the ball leaving his hand, fifty thousand fans rising to their feet, the jet stream of his fastball streaking past the baffled batter.

"Steee-rike three!" Zack the umpire yelled. "You're outta here!"

Zack did a funky potato-masher dance while his imaginary teammates stormed out of the dugout to mob him. He dropped to his knees, flopped sideways on the floor, and started spinning around in kicking circles.

"Zack Jennings wins the World Series! He wins the World Series!"

Stop that!

Zack froze. His eyes darted around the empty room. "Mom?"

He thought he heard her, knew it was impossible. "Mom?"

Zack stood, brushed off his pants, backed away from the archway where the living room connected to the dining room. He turned and faced a bay window. He looked across the street. The brownstone on the other side of West 84th Street. She was over there waiting for him, right above the front door—the monster with the sunken stone eyes.

"Wherever you go, whatever you do, I'll know," his mother had always told him. "I have eyes everywhere!"

A gargoyle. Logically, rationally, Zack knew that's all the monster across the street was. It wasn't alive and it certainly couldn't see. It was a figment of some stone carver's wild imagination. This one depicted a sad-faced lady with hair that grew into a thorny tangle of branches and leaves, what they called a Green Lady, half human, half tree. Her wide-open eyes were, in reality, deep holes bored with a mason's drill. But the irrational part of Zack's brain told him that the Stone Lady had seen him rolling around on the floor in his wedding clothes. She knew Zack had ruined another day for everybody else because he was so silly, so selfish. And the Stone Lady always reported everything to his mother.

"Mom?"

Zack and his dad had a big apartment for New York. Three bedrooms. A living room, a kitchen, and a dining room. Two and a half baths. The dining room was the only room in the whole apartment that terrified Zack.

The room right in front of him.

From the living room you step into the dining room— also known as the dying room.

It was empty. No boxes. No furniture. Nothing but the same stale smell: a dozen wet ashtrays leaching out of the walls.

Zack felt his heart race, felt it try to jump out of his chest and gallop down the hall so it could hide underneath his bed and tremble in the darkness. But there was no bed in the bedroom anymore. The moving men had broken it down and wrapped the frame pieces together with strapping tape so they could haul it up to Connecticut. Zack's heart would have to stay with him and face whatever was in the dying room.

"Mom?" Zack whispered. "I'm sorry, Mom."

His voice rang off walls where nothing remained except the cigarette smoke–stained outlines of picture frames. But sometimes Zack thought he could still see her—sick and swallowed up by the tilting bed. Skinny as a skeleton, bald from all the chemotherapy the cancer doctors had given her.

"I didn't even get all that dirty, honest. . . ."

Liar!

"I didn't mean to. . . ."

You're the reason I left. You're why I can't live with your father anymore. You're why I died. I had to leave so I could get away from you.

"I'm sorry, Mom."

The dining room had been empty for over a year. He and his father hardly ever came in here. Not since the medical-equipment company came and took away the hospital bed and the rolling medicine cabinet and the IV poles and the suction machine and the steel-framed commode chair. Not since the night nurse took all the medicine bottles and flushed the pills and painkillers down the toilet. Not since the night his mother died.

"Zack?" His father was standing behind him. "What's up?"

"Nothing."

He placed a hand on Zack's shoulder. "You okay?"

"Yeah. Fine."

"You miss her, huh?"

Zack knew he needed to choose his words very carefully. "Yes, Dad. I miss Mom."

"Me too. But, well, we talked about this, remember?"

"Yes, sir."

His father tousled Zack's hair. He had given the correct answer—he'd be back to play again tomorrow.

"Where's your tie?"

Zack pulled a clip-on bow tie out of his tuxedo jacket. It was purple, his new stepmother's favorite color.

"Hey, how'd your tux get so dirty?" His father

swiped some lint off Zack's back. "You don't want to spoil our big day, do you?"

"No, sir."

"Great. Well, I guess we shouldn't keep everybody waiting. . . ."

His father smiled, Zack pretended to smile back, and the two of them marched out of the apartment.

Zack knew his father was excited, eager to start his brand-new life.

Zack also knew that, given half a chance, he'd probably ruin this one for his dad, too.

3

Judy Magruder helped set up the champagne glasses for the wedding toast.

She stacked the slender flutes in a tenuous pyramid atop the linen-covered table set up in one corner of the apartment building's rooftop garden.

"Is that too tall?" she asked a waitress.

"No, that looks—"

Before the waitress could say "fine," a gust of wind whipped up the side of the building. For a brief instant, the delicate glasses became long-necked dragonflies suspended on the breeze. Gravity, however, soon took over and the glasses crash-landed on the patio's concrete pavers.

"Oops."

It was a good thing Judy was the bride today. She'd tell you herself: Her very presence seemed capable of causing glassware to leap off table ledges like lemmings on a family vacation to the Grand Canyon.

Dressed in her billowy purple wedding gown, Judy crouched down and started searching for shattered glass.

She quickly found the first shard. "Ouch. Be careful," she said to the waiter and waitress helping her clean up. "You could cut yourself."

Proving her point, she sucked the fingertip she'd just cut. Deciding she'd better check underneath the table, too, she jounced forward, scrunched up tufts of taffeta, and scooted through an opening in the table linens like they were curtains and she was going backstage after taking her bows, something she had done when she'd been an actress. That was before she published the first book in her series about Curiosity Cat, a white tabby with gray paws who, as the name suggested, was extremely curious and, consequently, always in trouble. Most of Judy's friends and family said her children's books were all semiautobiographical.

Judy crawled forward and discovered she wasn't alone under the table. "Hey, Zack. Whatcha doin' down here?"

Zack twisted the plastic arms of a G.I. Joe. "Nothing."

"Good. Sometimes nothing is the best thing to do on crazy days like this." She lofted a strand of hair out of her eyes by blowing sideways through her lips. "That a firefighter?" she asked.

Zack looked at the doll and nodded, even though he was embarrassed. A boy his age playing with dolls? Youch.

"That's G.I. Joe, right?"

Again, Zack nodded. "Yeah."

"Hi, Mr. Joe," Judy said.

"Howdy, ma'am." She did Joe's voice, too. Rugged and tough.

"Hey, Zack?" Judy asked.

"Yeah?"

"Do you think Mr. Joe can handle hazmats?"

"What's a hazmat?"

"You know—hazardous materials? You just kind of chop the words off and squish them back together. Haz-mats."

"Oh. I dunno."

"Lives are at stake. Toes, too."

Zack stared at Judy. He was still trying to figure this lady out. Sure, she was pretty and his dad laughed a lot whenever he and Judy were together. Judy laughed, too, because Zack's dad was almost remembering how to be funny again. Her books about the cat were kind of okay. Zack had read a couple, even though they were mostly for little kids. Still, they were kind of funny. Especially when Curiosity Cat got into trouble poking his nose into places he shouldn't. One time, he even blew himself up, but because he has nine lives it didn't really matter.

And Zack had never heard Judy yell at his dad, not once.

Not yet, anyway.

"It's a pretty serious situation out there," said Judy. "We're talking broken glass. Open-toed sandals. Things could get ugly."

Zack looked into Judy's eyes. She had big brown ones, the kind you see on friendly cartoon bears—the ones you can trust, not the growly, grizzly types you can't.

He played along. "Mr. Joe?" he said to the action figure.

"Yeah, Zack?" Judy grunted back.

"Um, have you ever worked hazmat duty before?"

"Hazmat? Sure, sure. All the time. I'm fearless. I'm also plastic, so, you know, I can't get injured unless, you know, I melt or a fire truck backs over me. That'll hurt."

A smile stole across Zack's face.

"Ask Joe if he's ever had to deal with broken glass."

"Okay. Hey, Joe?"

"Yeah?"

"You ever work with glass?"

"Glass? Schmass. Can't cut me, pal. Well, it could, but I wouldn't, you know, bleed or nothin'."

"Because you're made out of plastic, right?"

"Exactly!"

Zack laughed. Judy, too.

George Jennings and Judy Magruder were married the Saturday before Memorial Day. Zack Jennings was his father's best man and official ring bearer.

After their rooftop wedding reception, the new family flew to Orlando for a weeklong honeymoon and vacation at Walt Disney World. While they were in Orlando, the moving company would clean out their apartments and truck everything up to North Chester, Connecticut, the small town where George had grown up.

Their new house, a just-built three-story Victorian—with gables and a wraparound porch—was located in the brand-new Rocky Hill Farms subdivision west of town.

Right near the crossroads where County Route 13 meets Connecticut State Highway 31.

4

Every Monday morning, Gerda Spratling rode into North Chester like her family still owned the town.

Her chauffeur would pilot her 1952 Cadillac Coupe DeVille down the center of Main Street. A few cars would honk their horns at the big black boat straddling the solid yellow line, but the locals simply moved out of the way. They recognized the antique automobile and knew that inside was the sole surviving member of the family that had made North Chester famous. In fact, the quaint little town was still called Clocksville, as it had been for nearly a century, because of the timepieces once mass-produced in the sprawling Spratling Clockworks Factory.

"Spratling Stands the Test of Time," their ads used to say. But the redbrick factory with its colossal smokestacks had been shuttered since the early 1980s.

Since this particular Monday morning was also Memorial Day, tourists and townspeople were lazily enjoying the unofficial start of summer by poking around Main Street's shops and cozy boutiques.

"Why aren't these people at work?" Miss Spratling asked her driver.

"It's a holiday, ma'am." The chauffeur was eighty-six years old. Miss Spratling was seventy-two.

"Holiday? God in heaven. Lazy, shiftless layabouts." Her voice was sharp and brittle.

The car coasted to a stop.

"Why are we stopping?" Miss Spratling demanded.

"Red light, ma'am."

"God in heaven."

Downtown North Chester had only one stoplight—at the intersection where the town clock, a massive stone tower, also stood. Miss Spratling's great-grandfather had commissioned the six-story fieldstone monument to commemorate his family's Germanic ingenuity and American industriousness. The clock had ornately scrolled hands and a filigree face, but it no longer told time. The hands stood frozen at 9:52.

The light changed.

"Hurry along, Mr. Willoughby," Miss Spratling ordered from the backseat. "Hurry along."

"Yes, ma'am."

Miss Spratling had two standing appointments in town every Monday. First the beauty parlor, then the florist. Her personal assistant, a young woman named Sharon Jones, followed the Cadillac in a Hyundai hatchback, just in case Miss Spratling should require anything at all. The Cadillac had bullet-shaped bumper guards, tail fins, and a massive chrome grill and was kept in mint condition by Mr. Willoughby, the gaunt and gangly chauffeur.

The two cars parked in the No Parking zone alongside the curb in front of Mr. Antoine's House of Beauty. Mr. Willoughby shuffled around the car to open Miss Spratling's door. The skinny assistant stood with bowed head and slumped shoulders at the curb.

"Wait for me. Both of you."

Miss Spratling would have her hair done by Mr. Antoine himself—even on a holiday. The hairdresser was years younger, but he knew the old-fashioned way to curl her limp locks, using rollers the size of coffee cans and a helmet-shaped hair dryer—the kind beauty parlors had back in the 1950s.

After her hair appointment, Miss Spratling was driven up Main Street to Meade's Flower Shoppe, where she would purchase one dozen white roses. She had purchased the same thing every Monday for nearly fifty years. Her assistant came into the store with her because it was Sharon's job to actually carry the thorny roses.

This Monday, Meade's was unexpectedly crowded.

"Miss Spratling! So good to see you again!"

"Mr. Meade." She tugged on her elbow-length black gloves and slid her cat's-eye glasses up the bridge of her nose. "Who are all these people?"

"It's Memorial Day, ma'am."

"So?"

"They've come in to buy flowers to take out to the graveyards."

"I see. Need a federal holiday to remember the dead, do they? Where were these people *last* Monday?"

Mr. Meade nodded sympathetically. "You know, Miss Spratling, I was just asking myself the same thing."

"Enough chatter. Move along. Bring us our roses."

"I'll be right with you. Mrs. Lombardi needs—"

"We haven't the time to wait." Miss Spratling moved forward, her hands clasped behind her back. "You know what we require. Either produce it immediately or next Monday we will be forced to make alternative arrangements."

"Yes, Miss Spratling. . . . Of course, Miss Spratling. . . ."

The florist skittered away. An elderly woman in a faded Windbreaker smiled at Miss Spratling. She was clutching a bouquet of red, white, and blue carnations.

"They're for my Arnie," she said.

"What?"

"The carnations. They're for my son. He died in the war. I take him flowers every Memorial Day."

"I see. That makes it easier to remember, doesn't it?

The federal holiday." Miss Spratling fussed with her hard helmet of hair. The woman in the Windbreaker stared at her.

"God in heaven, woman, whatever are you gawking at?"

"That dress. I had one just like it. Years ago. When Mr. Lombardi and I went to our first formal at his fraternity. Must have been 1948."

Miss Spratling wanted to be left alone. "Mr. Meade?" she called out.

"Of course Mr. Lombardi passed on. Last year. Congestive heart failure. I'm all alone now. I do the best I can. Stay busy. Volunteer at the thrift shop . . ."

"Mr. Meade?" Miss Spratling rapped her knuckles on the counter.

"My dress was white," Mrs. Lombardi said. "Not black like yours."

"Mr. Meade!"

The frazzled shopkeeper came hurrying out of the back room with a dozen white roses wrapped in a cone of clear cellophane.

"Kindly charge them to my account," Miss Spratling snapped as her assistant took the flowers from the frightened little man.

Mr. Meade smiled feebly. "Of course. No problem, Miss Spratling. Have a nice day."

"How sweet of you to suggest such a thing," she coldly replied. "Unfortunately, I have not had, as you say, a 'nice day' for nearly fifty years!"

The two cars crawled out of North Chester and headed up Route 13. A few miles outside of town, both vehicles parked on the soft shoulder of the road.

Mr. Willoughby once again shuffled around to the rear of the Cadillac and pulled open the heavy door. Miss Spratling snatched the roses out of her assistant's hands and carried the bouquet as though it were her wedding day. She crossed over the drainage ditch and made her way up a well-worn path until she came to a gigantic oak tree.

There was a white wooden cross nailed into the tree. It had hung there so long, swollen bark had grown in around its edges. A small aluminum bucket, also painted white, was bolted to the tree underneath the cross. It was filled with a dozen wilted white roses, their tissue-thin edges rimmed brown with a week's decay.

Miss Spratling did what she did every Monday: She tossed out last week's dead roses and put the fresh ones in. She pressed her left hand against the furrowed bark and said some prayers.

Five minutes later, she made her way back to the waiting car. Her assistant met her at the crumbling edge of the roadway.

"We have done our duty, Sharon."

"Yes, ma'am."

"Take me home, Mr. Willoughby."

"Yes, ma'am," said the ancient chauffeur.

The Cadillac drove away. Miss Spratling would come back again the next Monday and the next one and the one after that. Every week, she'd bring fresh white roses to decorate her roadside memorial at the crossroads where Route 13 met Highway 31.

5

"The Tree of Life has three hundred and twenty-five images of endangered and extinct animals carved into its trunk, roots, and branches," said Judy.

On Memorial Day, Zack, Judy, and George—the whole new Jennings family—wound their way around the fourteen-story-tall man-made baobab tree that was the centerpiece to Disney's Animal Kingdom amusement park.

"It's awesome!" Zack stared up at all the animals etched into the fake tree like a gigantic interlocking jig-saw puzzle.

"Can you see the lion?" his father asked. "In the bark there? I think it's a lion. Maybe a leopard. I know it's not a panda bear. . . ."

"Yeah. Cool." Zack had been having a blast in Orlando and figured his new stepmom could turn out to be a whole lot more fun than his real mom.

That's when he smelled her, smelled the cigarette.

His mother.

Zack imagined she had come back from the dead to teach him a lesson. How dare he have fun with his pretty new stepmother when his real mother was dead on account of him? This wasn't the Tree of Life. It was the Tree of Death!

"Zack?" his dad asked. "Are you okay?"

He nodded. Tried to speak. "Yeah. Fine."

Judy sniffed the air. She smelled it, too.

"Somebody's smoking," she said.

"I thought the whole park was nonsmoking." Zack's dad sounded mad.

"It is," said Judy. "But you know smokers. They have trouble reading signs." Now Judy looked at Zack. She must have seen the panic in his eyes. "You okay, hon?" she asked softly.

"Yeah. Thanks."

Zack knew smokers, too. Lived with one most of his life. His mother went through two or three packs a day. Sucked on them hard, like she wanted to drain each stick dry. His mother kept smoking until the day she died, even though the cigarettes were what caused the cancer.

"They're the only joy I have left," she used to croak from that hospital bed in the dining room. She would stare at Zack with a look that seared his soul deeper than the glowing tip of a cigarette could scorch his skin. "My only joy in the world."

6

Gerda Spratling lived in the one true mansion near North Chester, Connecticut: Spratling Manor.

Her great-great-grandfather Augustus J. Spratling, the founder of Spratling Clockworks, had built the stately stone castle in 1882 on one thousand forested acres six miles west of town. Miss Spratling had lived in the manor her entire life. When her father died in 1983, he left her the house and a handsome inheritance. Her mother had died years earlier, when Gerda was an infant.

It had been twenty-five years since her father had passed away, and the money was starting to run out. Still, she had enough to live on, provided she lived frugally. She sold off some of the land, trimmed the staff to three, shut down parts of the mansion, and kept most of the rooms upstairs locked or boarded shut.

Miss Spratling had moved her bedroom furniture

into what had once been the library, a mahogany-paneled chamber entered through colossal sliding doors and connected by a secret passageway to the Spratling family chapel.

The area around her island of bedroom furniture was empty save for her father's old rolltop desk and the dusty bookshelves climbing up the towering walls.

There was a rolling stepladder resting against the tallest bookcase. No one had ascended it for twenty-five years, not since Miss Spratling's father had climbed to its top, noosed a braided curtain pull around his neck, kicked the ladder aside, and fallen just far enough to snap his neck and die.

Miss Spratling's personal assistant, Sharon, slept in the walk-in pantry off the kitchen so she would be close at hand should her employer require anything during the night.

Sharon's mother, a chambermaid who had worked for the Spratlings for many decades, lived in a ramshackle carriage house down one of the winding drives coursing through the estate's overgrown grounds. Mrs. Jones roomed there so Miss Spratling would not have to listen to the screaming infant the woman took care of: Sharon's baby boy.

A little before midnight, Sharon awoke to see a black silhouette standing in her doorway.

"Sharon, we have run out of Frangelico. Sharon?"

Sharon's name always had a much longer "ssshhh" at the front of it on Monday nights when Miss Spratling had been drinking. The weekly visits to the memorial made the old woman sad, and sadness made her drink more than usual. Frangelico was Miss Spratling's favorite alcoholic beverage: a sweet and syrupy concoction that tasted like a hazelnut milk shake, except that it burned your throat.

"Sharon? God in heaven! Wake up, girl!"

"Yes, ma'am," Sharon mumbled.

"You must go to the store immediately!"

Sharon knew no liquor store would be open at this hour, so she would need to improvise. She sleepwalked to the curtained shelves where she kept her work clothes.

"Hurry along, girl! Lay a patch, as they say."

Sharon drove over to the Mobil station on Highway 31. They were open twenty-four hours and had a mini-market that sold coffee. At the counter with the Styrofoam cups and plastic lids were tubs of flavored nondairy creamer. One was called Hazelnut Delight, which sort of tasted like Frangelico, especially if you never saw the tiny tubs. She'd bring home a few dozen, empty them into a glass, and add some whiskey.

"Just the coffee?" asked the checkout clerk.

"And the creamers."

"Did she run out of Frangelico again?"

Sharon nodded.

"You sure you have enough?"

"Yes."

Sharon pulled out a wrinkled dollar bill.

"Coffee's free tonight," said the clerk. "Creamers, too."

"Really?"

The clerk winked. "Yes, ma'am. Happy Memorial Day."

"Thank you."

Sharon scooped up the creamer tubs and slipped them into the pockets of her smock. She wasn't a nurse, but Miss Spratling insisted that she wear a uniform. She hurried out to her car. It was well past midnight.

She drove away from the gas station and reached the darkest stretch of highway. No strip malls. No houses. No lights. Just the dark forest lining both sides of the road, the treetops becoming a dense stockade fence, running their jagged tips against the inky sky. Sharon had the road to herself, except for the moths and bugs intent on dive-bombing into her headlights. She flicked on the radio but heard nothing except static.

She looked down.

Weird.

She'd never had radio trouble in this spot before. Even at night.

Weird.

She looked up from the control console to the road.

"Oh, no!"

There was a girl standing in the middle of the road. A girl dressed all in white.

Sharon slammed on her brakes. The front end of the car swerved left; the rear end skidded right.

Sharon's heart thumped against her chest.

She tried to breathe.

Her front bumper was only two inches away from the girl in white.

I could've killed her.

A smile blossomed on the girl's placid face as she made her way over to the passenger-side window. She seemed to glow, to carry her own aura of throbbing red light. Then Sharon realized she had come to a stop at the crossroads, with its blinking red stoplight.

"I wonder if I might trouble you for a ride?" the girl asked.

"What?"

"I'm terribly late."

She could also be terribly mental, thought Sharon. *Standing in the middle of the highway like that.*

"Where are you going?" Sharon asked.

"Down the road. I'm late."

The girl in white was a teenager. Sixteen, maybe seventeen. Her soft blond hair was tied back in a ponytail by a white chiffon scarf. She wore a stiff white dress that was snug around her slender waist. She had on long white gloves. A white shawl was draped over her bare shoulders. She was white on white on white.

She'd also get creamed if she kept standing in the middle of the road.

"Hop in," said Sharon.

The girl in white waited outside.

"Could you open the door, please?"

"What?"

"It's these silly white gloves. I'd sure hate to sully them."

Reluctantly, Sharon leaned across the seat and opened the door.

"Thanks! You're the most!" Her gown rustled as she slid into the car.

"Um," said Sharon, "we really can't go anywhere until you close your door."

"Do you mind doing it for me?"

"What?"

The seated girl showed Sharon her white gloves again.

"Right," Sharon mumbled. "Wouldn't want you to 'sully' them, would we?"

As Sharon leaned across the teenager's lap to grab the door handle, she felt a strange chill. Goose bumps exploded on her arm.

The girl in white just giggled. "Come on! Let's lay a patch and wail!"

=   =   =

The little car hummed along for about a mile. The girl in white sat silently and stared straight ahead. More moths threw themselves at Sharon's high beams. Others went for her windshield.

"So, where are you headed?" Sharon finally asked.

"Down the road."

"I know. But where? North Chester? Monroe?"

"Down the road."

"This road's awfully long."

"I'm going to the dance. At Chumley Prep."

Sharon felt her stomach twist into knots. "Chumley?"

"Yes. My boyfriend invited me down for their summer social."

"Chumley?"

"Yes." The girl looked at her delicate wristwatch. "We should just make it. The dance won't start until eight."

Sharon tasted something sour rising up into her throat. "Uh, you know, it's already after midnight."

"Oh, dear. Midnight?"

"Yeah."

"Why didn't you come along sooner?"

The girl in white wasn't smiling anymore. In fact, she looked ready to snarl. So Sharon decided it was her turn to stare straight ahead.

"Maybe you made a mistake," Sharon said to the windshield, hoping to calm her passenger's quick-trigger temper. "You know that school? Chumley Prep? They closed that down years ago. Back before I was even born."

She dared to look over at the girl in white.

But she wasn't there.

The passenger seat was empty.

7

On Tuesday, the day after Memorial Day, a tanker truck traveled down County Route 13, hauling its load of fresh milk to the dairy-processing plant on the far side of North Chester.

It hissed and clicked its air brakes as it came to a stop at the crossroads. The driver looked up at the blinking red stoplight, glanced out both side windows, and checked for traffic coming in either direction on Highway 31.

Then his windshield exploded.

A tree limb slammed through the glass and pinned him to his seat like a prized trophy in a butterfly collection.

The branch had come from a gigantic oak tree that towered over the intersection.

An oak tree with a white wooden cross nailed into its trunk.

8

"This, of course, is Main Street," Zack's father said as they drove through North Chester.

It was Monday, a week after Memorial Day. After their vacation in Florida, the Jennings family was ready to move into their new Connecticut home. They drove up Main Street, which had so many old-fashioned-looking storefronts and cast-iron lampposts, it reminded Zack of that other Main Street—the fake one down in Disney World.

"There's the town clock!" Zack called from the backseat. "See it?"

Because Zack and his father sometimes came up to North Chester to visit his grandpa, Zack knew all the tourist sites worth pointing out.

"Wow! That's neat," said Judy.

Zack and Judy and Zack's father had had a blast down in Mouse Land. Riding rides, telling stories, laughing. His dad was loosening up, so Zack did, too. He let silly stuff tumble out of his mouth without being afraid that his mother might scream at him for being such an immature baby. His stepmother, Judy, seemed to enjoy his "flights of fancy"—that's what she called it when Zack made stuff up.

"I've never seen a clock so big," Judy remarked. "How do they wind it?"

"They don't," said Zack's father. "It rusted out years ago. So no matter what train you take, it's always the 9:52."

"Yeah, but in the old days," said Zack, "they used to have these monkeys and squirrels inside to wind it."

Judy laughed. "Monkeys?"

"And squirrels," Zack added. "Grandpa told me."

"My father, like so many Jennings men, was prone to exaggeration," said George.

"Well, be that as it may, I'd like to hear about these furry little timekeepers."

"Okay," said Zack. "The guys in charge of the clock—"

"The clockmeisters," his father added.

"Right, the clockmeisters would put bananas and walnuts up in the top of the tower, up above all the gears and pulleys and stuff. Then they'd open the cages and the monkeys and squirrels would climb up the gear teeth to get at the food."

"Gears have teeth?" Judy asked.

"Grandpa said that's why they needed a dentist to live inside the clock."

"I see. . . ."

"Anyway, they'd climb up the teeth and that made the gears turn and that wound the clock."

"Fascinating."

"Grandpa knew the dentist. They played poker on Tuesdays."

Zack's father pulled the car into a parking lot fronting what looked like a fairy-tale cottage made of weathered brick and topped by a steeply sloped slate roof.

"And this is where my dad used to work," he said.

"This was the police station?" Judy marveled. "It's beautiful."

"True. It's also old. And drafty, especially in the winter. So the town built the guys a brand-new municipal building a little ways up the road."

"But, ma'am," Zack said to Judy with a thick cowboy twang, "when my grandpa rode the range, this here was the hoosegow where he locked up all them cattle rustlers and train robbers."

"He wrote a lot of traffic tickets," Zack's father gently corrected him. "Rescued cats out of trees. Come on, Zack—we don't need to embellish *everything*."

Zack sank back into his seat. "Yes, sir."

= = =

They picked up a few sacks of groceries at the market on Main Street, then headed out to see their new house.

"Wow," said Judy.

She was admiring the scenery. Rolling hills. Stone fences. The whole state of Connecticut looked like the cover of a Christmas card, only it was summer now, so there wasn't any sparkle-flake snow on the ground.

"That's the entrance to Spratling Manor," Zack's father said when they neared a pockmarked driveway leading to a wrought iron gate.

"It's a haunted castle," said Zack. "Lots of evil lurks behind those walls."

"Really?" said Judy. "Evil? And it's lurking?"

"Yep. Grandpa said so, anyway." Zack pressed his nose against the window. "Coming up next is the field where the Rowdy Army Men roam. Late at night, you can see them marching out of the forest."

"Okay," said Judy. "Just exactly who are these Rowdy Army Men?"

"Dead soldiers from the Korean War," said Zack. "They got drunk and shot each other."

"Oh-kay. Any ghosts at our house?"

Probably just my dead mother, Zack wanted to say, but instead he mumbled, "I hope not."

Judy turned around. "Are you okay, hon?"

"Yeah."

"Here we are." His father eased to a stop at the red blinking light. "Home sweet home!"

Judy looked around. "We live in the middle of a highway?"

"No. We're right over there." Zack's father pointed to the far side of the intersection. "See?"

"No. Sorry. I see trees and a squirrel. Maybe he ran away from that clock tower."

Zack leaned forward. Good. No more ghost talk. They had jumped back to squirrels and monkeys.

"If you squint," he said, "you can kind of sort of see our chimney between all the trees."

Zack knew where the house was situated because he and his father had come up to watch the men building it one Saturday back in April while Judy was off on her *Curiosity Cat's Furball* book tour. This would be her first time seeing the house.

"It's right up there," he said. "See?"

"Yes. No. I'm lying. I don't see anything except trees. Wildflowers."

"Wait. How about that giant oak tree?" Zack's father pointed to a huge black tree. "The one with the white cross nailed to it."

"Okay. I can see the tree with the cross."

"That's us. That tree is in our backyard."

"Not another word!"

"But, Momma . . ."

"You'll get us both fired!"

Early that same Monday, Sharon was down at the Spratling Manor carriage house visiting her mother and son.

"I swear I saw her, Momma. Last week. The woman in white. The one folks talk about . . . right in the crossroads!"

"Do you want Miss Spratling to think you've gone mad?"

"I know what I saw, Momma."

The baby began to wail and kick.

"Now look what you've done. You woke up Aidan."

"I'm sorry, Momma."

"Sharon, you listen to me, girl: You are not to say another word about this. Not to anyone!"

"Yes, Momma."

An old intercom box mounted on the wall buzzed. Sharon's mother depressed the talk-back button.

"Yes, Miss Spratling?"

"Send Sharon up to the main house immediately!"

"Yes, Miss Spratling."

Sharon's mother took her finger off the button. "Hurry! Go!"

Sharon kissed Aidan goodbye and raced out the carriage house door.

It was another Monday.

Time to visit the roadside memorial.

10

Zack's father turned into the entrance of the Rocky Hill Farms subdivision.

The housing tract used to be a real farm until the farmer's family realized they could make more money selling the land than they could selling corn.

Most of the homes weren't quite finished. Tyvek-wrapped walls waited for vinyl siding. Two-by-fours and cinder blocks were stacked in the craggy dirt that one day would become front lawns.

They rounded a final curve and approached a huge house. A grand Victorian with five bedrooms and five baths. Even though it was brand-new, it looked like an old-fashioned gingerbread house.

"It's gorgeous," said Judy. "And huge!"

"Wait till you see the inside!" exclaimed Zack.

"Do we have a backyard?"

"Yep."

"I always wanted a backyard!" Judy hopped out of the car and ran off to find it. Halfway around the house, she stopped. "Guys? We have company."

Zack and his father hurried over to where they could see what Judy saw: a police officer and two men in coveralls strolling through the wooded area bounding the edge of their backyard.

"Ben?" Zack's father called out to the police officer, a tall, thin man in a khaki uniform and Smokey the Bear hat.

"George?" the cop hollered back.

"Friend of yours?" Judy whispered.

"Yep," said Zack's father. "Sheriff Ben Hargrove. He was a rookie cop back when my dad was sheriff."

Hargrove came into the yard. The two men in coveralls followed.

"By golly, it's good to see you, George," Hargrove said. "I heard you might be coming home."

"Moving in today. So, what's up? What brings you out this way?"

"We're checking all the trees up and down Route 13. Looking for dead limbs. This your new house?"

"Yeah."

"Nice one. This your wife and son?"

"I'm sorry. Yes. Judy, Zack—this is Sheriff Ben Hargrove."

"Hi!" Judy held out her hand. Hargrove shook it. Zack slid behind his father's leg to hide.

"Shy guy, hunh?" Hargrove said.

"I think he's just a little overwhelmed. Been a busy couple weeks. Right, Zack?"

Zack nodded.

"So, what's up with the trees?" George asked.

"They're killing people," said the younger of the two men in coveralls as he ran his hand through his shaggy hair.

Zack peeked around his father's leg. He could see that Mr. Coveralls hadn't shaved in a couple of days. Probably hadn't showered, either. He sort of looked like a pirate or a mechanic.

"Of course, there's no way of knowin' which tree's doin' the killing. None of 'em will confess! Like talkin' to a stump!" He cracked himself up.

The other man in coveralls, the older one, said nothing.

"George, do you know Tony Mandica?" Sheriff Hargrove gestured toward the younger of the two men.

"No, I don't think we've ever met."

Mr. Coveralls stuck out his hand. "Well, I'm Tony. And this is my pop, Anthony."

The old man said nothing.

"We're Mandica and Son Tree Service. He's Mandica. I'm the son. Give us a call and we'll give you a quote on trimming up your trees." Mandica pulled a dirty business card out of his top pocket. It was coated with sawdust, stained with oil, and probably smelled like gasoline.

"I see," said Zack's father skeptically. "And how much might that cost?"

Mandica shrugged. "Depends on what we find."

"Should I hire lawyers? Or does the court assign each offending oak its own public defender?"

Sheriff Hargrove wasn't laughing. "We recently had two tree-related accidents out this way, George. Hate to have any more."

"Was there a storm?" Judy asked.

"No, Mrs. Jennings. No storm. On the Friday night before Memorial Day a tree limb broke off someplace high and tore down the blinker light out over the crossroads. Lucky for us, nobody was hurt before we got her fixed. Four days later, another branch in the same general vicinity busted through a milk-truck driver's windshield. Killed him."

"One of our trees?" Zack's father asked, suddenly as serious as the sheriff.

"No way to know for certain. All we know is that it was an oak. Plenty of those on both sides of the road."

"Okay. We'll trim whatever you think needs trimming."

"Give me a call," said the younger Mandica, "and we'll set up an inspection."

"It won't come down," the old man suddenly said.

His son laughed. "What, Pop?"

"The tree. No man nor ax can pierce its bark."

"Oh-kay, Pop. Don't worry, folks. No matter what *he* says, six of my guys with chain saws can handle any tree you got. Come on, Pop. Let's go home and have a nice nap."

The two Mandicas disappeared into the trees edging the yard.

Zack remembered the tree near the museum in New York City. It was an oak, too. He wondered if the oak trees killing people up here were that tree's country cousins.

"We should go inside," Zack's father announced.

"Good to have you back in town, George," said Sheriff Hargrove.

"Thanks, Ben. Good to be home."

Hargrove waved goodbye and followed the Mandicas.

Zack's father went back to the car to grab the groceries.

Zack stared up at the canopy of tangled branches overhead.

"Woo-woo! Killer trees," said Judy in a funny, spooky voice. "Hey, Zack—do you think they're related to the killer bees?"

She was trying to make a joke.

Zack wasn't laughing.

11

The scruffy little dog heard the back door open and scampered into the kitchen.

"Who's this?" Zack asked when the dog sat down at his feet and raised a paw.

"Zack," said his dad, "meet Zipper!"

"Uh, hello," Zack said as he bent down to shake hands with Zipper.

Judy rubbed behind the dog's ears. Zipper rolled over on the floor to let her know he really needed his belly scratched right now, not his ears.

"Does he belong to a neighbor?" asked Zack.

"Nope," said his father. "He's your new dog!"

Zipper started yapping.

"Surprise!" said Judy.

"We figured you'd want a dog!" said his father.

"No, I don't."

"Sure you do!" his father insisted. "Out here in the country, every boy has a dog. In fact, I think it's a Connecticut state law. And just so you wouldn't get arrested, Dr. Freed, my old vet up here, let us have this great Jack Russell. He was the runt of the litter, so nobody wanted to adopt him. I asked Dr. Freed to drop him off this morning."

"Well, I think he's perfect," said Judy.

Zipper stood up on his hind legs.

"Did he do that on purpose?" Zack wondered out loud.

"I dunno," said Judy. "Let's see if he'll do it again. Up, Zipper! Up!"

The dog stood up again. This time, he twirled.

"You know what?" said Zack. "I think we should probably keep him. Especially if it's a state law and all."

About ten seconds after they'd gone into the house and done the whole welcome-to-Connecticut-here's-your-new-dog deal, Zack's father's high-tech DingleBerry (that was what Zack called it) cell phone started beeping on his belt, so he disappeared into the room already set up by the moving company to be his home office—the one with the bookshelves crammed with law books.

Judy and Zack went into the kitchen, where she attempted to toast bread for sandwiches. After she burned the first four slices and set off the smoke detector, Zack said he really didn't need toast for his sandwich; plain bread would be fine. When the smoke cleared, they moved into the breakfast nook.

Zipper followed after them, carrying what was, apparently, his favorite ball: a chewed-up spongy thing soaked with saliva. The dog curled up underneath Zack's stool to feast on foam rubber while the humans settled in with their bologna-and-yellow-mustard-on-plain-bread sandwiches.

"Did you ever eat your lunch in a breakfast nook before?" Judy asked Zack between bites.

"Nope."

"We don't have a lunch nook, do we?"

"I don't think so. But we have a dining room. . . ."

"Yeah, but I think that's only for dinner."

"This house is so huge," said Zack, "maybe we have a lunchroom somewhere. Like at school." He dropped a pinch of bologna down to Zipper, who gladly gave up his ball to snag it.

"That'd make a good story, wouldn't it?" Judy said. "A boy who has a cafeteria in his house instead of a kitchen? He lives in a *school*house with Curiosity Cat."

Zack joined in. "And the front hall is the study hall! And a hall upstairs is the detention hall!"

"Great idea, Zack. Can I steal it?"

"Sure," he said. "Just don't tell Curiosity Cat we got a dog."

After lunch, Zack's father came into the backyard to join Judy, Zack, and Zipper. Judy was throwing the spongy ball; Zipper was chasing it.

"How's it going?" his dad asked Zack.

The two of them were sort of alone, standing close to the back porch, watching Judy play with Zipper.

"Pretty good, I guess."

"I think you'll really like it up here. I know I did when I was your age."

"Yeah."

"Do you know why I wanted us to move up here, Zack?"

Zack didn't answer. He figured it was one of those rhetorical-type questions his father liked to ask so he could answer it himself.

"Well, I'll tell you."

Yep. It was one of those.

"I think you and I both need a chance to start over. A chance to do some of the things we couldn't do while, you know . . . before."

"Yeah."

All of a sudden, Zack wondered if his dad had to deal with the same ghosts he did. If so, maybe his father was right—maybe they could both have more fun in a place where his mother couldn't bother them because she was stuck back in New York City haunting that stupid dining room!

"You sure you like the dog?"

"Are you kidding? He's awesome! I mean, look how fast he is! He just zips! Zipper's the perfect name for him!"

Now the dog padded over and dropped the slobbery ball at Zack's feet instead of Judy's.

"Looks like he wants *you* to throw it," his father said.

"Really?"

"Yep. I believe our new friend has already heard who has the fastest fastball in all the major leagues!"

Zack smiled. Long ago, in the olden days, before his mother got sick, back when she'd leave the apartment to go clothes shopping all day, Zack and his dad used to goof around together. They'd play make-believe baseball or build LEGO robots. One time, they even made this fort out of cardboard boxes and . . .

The cell phone hooked to his father's belt began to beep again.

He, of course, took the call.

"Hello? No. No problem. I have those files up here with me. . . ."

Now the phone inside the house started to ring, too.

"Hang on," Zack's father said to the DingleBerry cell phone, which sort of looked like a calculator but with five hundred buttons. "Judy?" he called out. "You should probably grab that. It might be the library."

"The library?"

He nodded. "I let them know their favorite world-famous children's author was moving to town. They said they'd call to set up a reading."

"Oh. Okay."

Zack's dad went back to his cell phone. "Don? Give me a second. I'm not at my desk. . . ." He wandered up the porch steps and into the house.

The kitchen phone kept jangling. Zack guessed the moving company hadn't been able to figure out how to hook up the answering machine.

"You ready to go inside?" Judy asked.

"Not yet," Zack said. Zipper sat at his feet, eager for another toss.

"Okay. Um . . ."

Zack could tell Judy wasn't sure what she was supposed to say in her new role as stepmother.

"Just, you know, stay in the yard," she said. "Where we can see you, okay?"

"No problem-o."

Judy smiled, then hurried in to answer the phone.

Zack smiled, too. His dad was right: This whole new family deal might work out okay, especially up here in ghost-free Connecticut!

Well, at least between phone calls.

Zack squeezed the slimy ball in his right fist.

"It all comes down to this. It's the bottom of the ninth. The pitcher makes sure his center fielder, the rookie they call the Zipper, is deep enough."

Zipper moved backward a few inches and wagged his tail.

"Here's the windup and the pitch!" Zack made the sound of a wooden bat cracking into a fastball. "It's going deep, deep, to center field." He arched back and heaved the rubber ball skyward.

He threw it too far.

Zipper charged into the woods. Zack could hear the ball ripping through leaves, heard Zipper scurrying through underbrush.

Then everything went quiet.

"Zipper?"

Zack moved toward the tree line.

"Zipper? Where are you, boy?"

Zack pushed his glasses up his nose and studied the woods fringing his new yard. He imagined there were snakes and lizards and lions and coyotes back in there. Bears, too.

"Zipper?"

Zack stepped into the cool shade. He moved through weeds and sticker bushes and brushed past branches. He saw the ball lying in a puddle of mud and heard a low rumble. Growling.

"Zipper?"

Zipper yapped.

"There you are!"

The dog was snarling at a big black tree.

"Come here, boy."

Zipper wouldn't budge.

"Zipper? When I call you, you need to come, okay?" Zack pushed his way through a thicket.

An old lady dressed in black stepped out from behind the tree.

"Is this your dog?"

Zack froze. Zipper snarled.

"Dog like that ought to be kept on a leash."

"I don't think we have a leash yet. . . ."

"You can wrap a rope around his scrawny little neck, for all I care. Now, scoot. Skedaddle. This is my tree. And don't you dare let that mangy little mongrel piddle against it, you hear me, boy?"

"Yes, ma'am."

Zack saw the white cross nailed to the tree, the white flowers crammed into a rusty-bottomed bucket.

"Why are you still here?"

"I . . ." He glanced sideways, down the sloping embankment to the highway, where he saw an old man standing like a tired tin soldier near a big black car.

"Speak up, boy!"

"I was just looking at the cross."

"You're not to touch it! Ever!"

Zack realized who this scary old lady was: the Wicked Witch of the West. And this must be one of her enchanted trees—the ones that grew in the forest where Dorothy found the Tin Man.

"Do you understand me?"

"Yes, ma'am!"

Zack and Zipper both turned and ran.

He fully expected the giant oak tree to start swinging its branches and tossing acorns at him. Maybe it would tear down the power lines and electrocute him. Maybe it would try to kill him with a pointy-tipped branch.

Maybe this was the King of all the Killer Trees in New York and Connecticut.

Zack ran faster.

The next morning, Zack stumbled out of bed and slogged across the soft carpet to his own private bathroom. Zipper, who had spent the night curled up against his legs, hopped off the bed and trotted after him.

"Good morning, Zipper." Zack yawned.

He opened the bathroom door and heard gurgling.

He also smelled something foul. Like a three-week-old hard-boiled egg soaked in vinegar.

He wondered if maybe he had given Zipper too much bologna yesterday. Maybe he shouldn't have let the dog lick his ice cream bowl after dinner, either. Maybe Zipper was lactose intolerant because, frankly, the bathroom smelled like somebody or something had spent the night in there farting.

Zack heard more gurgling. Maybe the whole house was farting.

The toilet seat chattered up and down and looked like the flapping bill of a porcelain pelican. With every flip of the lip, Zack heard more sloshing and bubbling in the bowl.

Then he saw brown chunky stuff come flowing out over the sides.

Gross.

Fortunately, there were two more bathrooms down the hall.

Zack just hoped those toilets weren't puking, too.

About once every month, Billy O'Claire, the plumber, went to visit his grandmother at the nursing home.

Billy called his grandmother Mee Maw. He called the place where she lived the Smelly Old Folks Home because both were true: The home smelled and so did the old folks living inside it. The home smelled like mashed potatoes mixed with mop water. The old folks smelled like dirty diapers.

Billy pulled into the empty parking lot. This was no assisted-living retirement village. This was a cinder-block dump with weeds and cigarette butts in the gravel pits that used to be gardens. But it was the best the twenty-five-year-old plumber could do for his sixty-seven-year-old grandmother, even though the crazy old coot had raised him since he was a baby.

Billy had picked up a box of Little Debbie Oatmeal

Creme Pies. Mee Maw loved them because they were soft and spongy and easy to eat without putting in her dentures.

Billy knew Mee Maw would be sitting in the cafeteria, so he headed that way. The vast room was quiet except for an old man plunking sour notes on a battered upright piano.

Billy saw Mee Maw sitting at a table far from the window. Mee Maw hated windows. She always thought somebody was on the other side, waiting to smash the glass and grab her.

"Hey, Mee Maw." His grandmother's white hair was flat across the back of her head, plastered in place by her pillow. Billy knew she spent most of her days in bed, staring up at the ceiling. She had lived that way most of her life. Alone and afraid.

"Who are you?" Mee Maw looked up from her tray when Billy sat down across from her.

"I'm your grandson. Billy. Remember?"

"Who?"

"Billy O'Claire."

"That's *my* name. O'Claire."

"I know, Mee Maw."

"My name is Mary. Mary O'Claire."

"That's right. I brought you oatmeal pies, Mee Maw."

"How sweet. Be a dear and open one for me."

"Yes, ma'am."

Billy pulled out a plastic-wrapped pie and tore into the wrapper with his teeth.

"He was here again. Last night."

"Who, Mee Maw?"

"The man at the window. He says he's going to kill me for what I meant to do."

"Is that so?" Billy said it with the enthusiasm of someone who had heard the same story over and over, every day, his whole life.

When Billy was a baby, barely three months old, he had been sent to live with his reclusive grandmother. Maybe she wasn't so bad back then. Maybe she even went outdoors. Billy couldn't remember. He went to Mee Maw's after his parents had been killed by a cop in what the newspapers called a "bungled blackmail scheme."

"How's your baby boy?" Mee Maw asked.

"Don't know," Billy answered sheepishly.

"You don't know?"

"No, ma'am." After the divorce, the judge gave Billy's ex full custody of their baby boy.

Mee Maw shook her head. "Like father, like son."

"I brought you some candy, too," Billy said. "Bag of them mints you like. Maybe you can fling 'em at the window if the bad man comes back tonight."

"Like father, like son."

Billy rose from the table. It was time to go.

"I'll see you next time, Mee Maw."

He kissed his grandmother on the top of her head. He sometimes wondered why he bothered coming out to visit the old woman, but the answer was simple: Mee Maw was the only family he had.

Except, of course, for my son.

But his ex-wife, Sharon, wouldn't let Billy anywhere near Aidan—no matter how many times he went over to where she worked to beg.

And Billy hated going to that place.

Spratling Manor gave him the creeps.

Tuesday afternoon, Judy drove to the North Chester Public Library. It was a two-story redbrick building with a small schoolhouse steeple. It looked like it had been built sometime after the war. The Revolutionary War.

Judy loved the aroma of libraries: the scent of copy-machine toner peppered with just a pinch of plastic from crinkly dust jackets.

"Ms. Magruder?" A sweet little lady with curly white hair and bright purple reading glasses was standing behind the front desk. "My, you look exactly like the photograph inside your book jackets!"

"Are you Mrs. Emerson?"

"Yes, dear. Kindly wipe your feet."

Okay. Maybe she's more feisty than sweet.

"I'm Jeanette Emerson," the librarian said. "No relation."

"To Ralph Waldo?"

"Is there another? I was delighted to hear that you and Georgie have moved back to town."

"Georgie?"

"That's what I called him when he was a bluebird."

"Georgie was a bluebird?"

"Yes. Four straight summers. The bluebirds always won. Read far more books than either the sparrows or the parakeets. That's why I wanted to meet you."

"You want to talk about birds?" Judy asked.

"We could do that if you like. I, however, was much more interested in ascertaining whether you might be available to read your latest book to this year's flock of Summer Library Campers."

"I'd love to."

"Excellent. We start up in a few weeks. July, actually."

"My July is wide open."

"Wonderful. So, where are you and Georgie living?"

"Rocky Hill Farms. We're right near the intersection of these two highways."

Mrs. Emerson nodded. "Route 13. Highway 31."

Judy remembered George's little landmark. "We're in the corner where the tree is."

"I see. But as you may have noticed, there are several trees on all sides of that particular intersection."

"We've got the one with the white cross."

"Ah, yes. Miss Gerda Spratling's *descanso*."

"Gerda . . ."

"Spratling. The family is of German descent. Gerda, I believe, means 'protector.' Her family, the Spratlings, ran the clock factory here for ages. Ran the town, too."

"What's a *descanso*?"

"Spanish word for roadside memorial. In the early days of the American Southwest, funeral processions would carry the coffin out to the graveyard for burial. From time to time, the pallbearers might set the casket down by the side of the road and rest. When the procession resumed, the priest would bless the spot where the deceased's soul had tarried on its final journey. The women would then scatter juniper flowers and stake a cross into the ground to further commemorate the site."

"So someone died behind our house? What was it? A car wreck?"

Mrs. Emerson hesitated.

"Ms. Magruder, might I be frank?"

"Please."

"That cross has been hanging on that old oak tree so long, I doubt if even Miss Spratling remembers why she hung it there."

"Well, that'll be my second investigation," Judy said.

"And your first?"

"Discovering why the town clock stopped."

"Ah, yes. There are several interesting stories about that. I'd tell you now, but I have to read Mother Goose to the children. Are you free for dinner this evening?"

=   =   =

The storm started about eight p.m.

Thunder boomed and the windows of the restaurant rattled. Judy didn't mind: Mrs. Emerson was an excellent storyteller. She regaled Judy with tales of a girl so ugly "her face could stop a clock." Apparently, she arrived by train in North Chester one day at exactly 9:52 p.m.

"Then there's the story of Osgood Vanderwinkle," Mrs. Emerson said.

"Who's he?"

"Clock keeper, dear."

"Did he have any monkeys or squirrels on his staff?"

"No. None that I'm aware of. However, he might have *seen* several—as well as assorted pink elephants. Mr. Vanderwinkle loved to tipple his rum. He was soused so often, we suspect he forgot to close the trapdoor at the top of the tower. The rains came . . ."

"The gears rusted?"

"Exactly. I suppose that story is the most mundane and, therefore, probably closest to the truth."

"Too bad."

"Indeed."

Around nine-thirty p.m. Judy said goodbye to Mrs. Emerson and ran across the muddy restaurant parking lot to her car.

She shivered and waited for the front and rear window defrosters to do their job. A twist of the wiper-control knob sent the windshield blades slapping back and forth to chase away the unrelenting rain. Judy cranked up the radio so she wouldn't have to listen to any more clouds explode.

She had called George earlier, told him about her dinner plans with Mrs. Emerson. He said, "Have fun. Drive carefully."

She had had fun.

Now she would try to drive carefully.

The radio was calling it a gully washer.

Flood warnings were in effect. Water rolled across the freeway in rippling waves. Wind gusted and made the treetops dance a wild, frenzied tango. The weatherman predicted that the storm would last until midnight with "the usual creeks overrunning their banks."

For an instant, Judy wished she still lived in New York City. In a high-rise apartment building. Someplace without creeks.

Then she heard a tire blow out.

The car skidded slightly and Judy carefully eased it off the road. She came to a stop right in front of an old graveyard about a quarter mile west of the crossroads. She could see the flashing red light blurring in the distance.

That meant George and home weren't far away. He could drive out in their other car and rescue her. She reached for her cell phone.

The battery was dead and she had forgotten the car adapter.

She looked up and down the highway. There was no traffic. No tow trucks cruising the highways she could flag down like a taxi in Times Square. There was nobody on the road at all.

Except, all of a sudden, Judy sensed somebody staring at her.

Somebody outside the car.

She turned slowly to the left. To the window.

She practically jumped out of her skin.

15

The storm moved closer.

Zack sat on his bed with Zipper, stared out the window, and counted the seconds between seeing lightning and hearing thunder.

"I used to be afraid of thunderstorms," he comforted his dog. "Now I just pretend it's somebody bowling in the clouds. A giant probably. And he uses the moon for his bowling ball."

Zack heard the familiar gurgling from behind his bathroom door. The rainwater was probably flooding the cracked sewer lines—sending more gunk upstairs to burble out of his toilet.

It was a good thing their new house had so many bathrooms. Zack's was currently off-limits and would be, his dad said, until the plumber showed up.

So Zack had rolled up a spare towel and jammed it into the crack at the bottom of the bathroom door.

He didn't want the odor oozing out to make his bedroom smell farty, too.

But what if the lightning moved too close and an electrical spark made all that trapped gas explode?

Zack tried not to look worried. He didn't want to scare his new dog. Besides, he'd already unpacked his G.I. Joe firefighter action figure—the one Judy said knew how to handle "hazmats," hazardous materials like sewer gas.

But Judy wasn't home.

If the bathroom blew, Zack would have to do all of Joe's voices himself.

16

There was a big burly man standing six inches from Judy's door.

"Howdy, ma'am," he said, oblivious to the slashing sheets of rain. "Car trouble?" His voice sounded muffled because Judy had kept all the windows rolled up tight. She feigned a smile and waved to signal she was fine, just fine.

"Front left tire," the man said. "She's blown."

The man wore some sort of navy blue uniform—so wet it looked black. Raindrops guttered off the bill of his cap—the kind milkmen and airplane pilots used to wear. There was an embroidered patch on its crown: Greyhound Scenicruiser. A name tag was pinned to his chest: Bud.

"Didn't mean to spook you," Bud said. "Do you require roadside assistance?"

Judy lowered her window. A crack.

"My name is Bud." He pointed to his name tag to prove it.

"I'm Judy. I've never had a flat before."

"Wish I could fix her for you. But I can't."

"Oh. Bad back?"

Bud didn't answer.

"I live just up the road," Judy said. "I was going to call my husband, but my phone died. Can I borrow yours?"

"My telephone?"

"Right. Can I borrow it?"

"Sorry, ma'am. I don't have a phone out here. They have one down at the filling station, if I remember correctly."

The rain pattered on his hat and shoulders.

"I could talk you through the tire change. Do you have a spare?"

"Yes. I think so. In the back."

Bud waited.

Judy had always considered herself a good judge of character. She hoped she was right because she judged Bud to be kind of spooky but not dangerous. Grabbing her tiny umbrella, she stepped out into the rain.

Bud stayed where he was.

"The jack's in the back," she said.

Rain blew sideways and the flimsy umbrella did little to keep Judy from getting drenched as she walked to the rear of the car. Bud followed. When the light from the emergency flashers hit his face, each burst made him appear ghoulish, like someone flicking a flashlight on and off underneath their chin.

Judy opened the hatchback and hoped Bud's bad back wouldn't prevent him from rolling the spare tire up to the front of the car.

Apparently, it did.

So she pushed it up the pavement with one hand while balancing her worthless umbrella in the other. Bud followed behind her. The way he dragged his feet, like his shoes were ill-fitting cinder blocks, Judy figured the guy's back must be *killing* him.

Bud talked Judy through the tire change. He told her what to do and Judy did it.

"Sorry I couldn't take care of the job myself," Bud said when the tire was changed.

"You helped plenty. Thanks!"

"Guess you owe me one."

"Guess so."

"Say—do you live around here?"

"Yes. See that tree with the cross? Down there near the intersection? Well, that tree is in our backyard."

"You don't say?"

"Yep."

"Sort of an eyesore, isn't it?"

"Excuse me?"

"The old wooden cross. The rusty bucket of dead flowers. It's an eyesore, all right."

"I guess."

"You folks ought to chop it down."

"The memorial?"

"The whole tree."

"Oh. Okay. I'll mention it to my husband." She climbed into her car.

"We'd appreciate it!" Bud snapped her a crisp two-finger salute.

Judy nodded and eased back onto the highway.

She wanted to reach the crossroads and turn the corner because every time she looked up at her rearview mirror, she saw Bud glimmering in her taillights—swinging his arms like he had an ax and was chopping down a tree.

17

"Sharon?"

Gerda Spratling stumbled around her bedchamber.

"Sharon? Where are you, girl?"

Miss Spratling found a small silver bell and shook it violently.

"Sharon!" She jangled the bell even harder.

Sharon slid open the panel doors.

The storm had torn down the power lines to Spratling Manor. The only illumination came from lightning flashing through the casement windows.

"Is everything all right, ma'am?"

Sharon carried a fluttering candle that sent shadows skipping across the cavernous room. The candlelight made everything in the creepy old house even creepier—especially Miss Spratling.

"Sharon, dearie, have I ever told you about Clint

Eberhart?" A girlish smile crept across the old woman's wrinkled lips. "Oh, he was the most. The absolute most. Thick, wavy hair. Such a dreamboat. Clint doesn't think I'm ugly. . . ."

"Can I bring you anything, ma'am?"

Thunder cracked. Glass rattled.

"Bring me champagne!"

Sharon tried to figure out what they sold at the gas station that might pass for champagne. Maybe ginger ale.

"No. Never mind. Clint will bring the bubbly! Daddy promised."

"Yes, ma'am. If you require nothing further . . ."

"Only that you be happy for me!"

Sharon backed away. Inched toward the door.

"Oh, Daddy!" Miss Spratling screamed. "You have made me the happiest little girl in the whole wide world!"

Boom! Another blast of thunder rocked the bedroom. Zipper whimpered.

"Hey, Zip—did you know that sound travels eleven thousand feet per second? And there are five thousand, two hundred and eighty feet per mile."

Lightning flashed.

"One Mississippi, two Mississippi, three Mississippi, four Mississippi, five—"

Thunder exploded.

"Okay, see? That lightning was less than a mile away, 'cause for every four point seven seconds between—"

The sky flared white. Thunder roared instantaneously with the flash. Then Zack heard an explosion—like a wooden crate being blown to bits by a stack of dynamite.

The lightning must've hit something in the backyard!

Zack and Zipper raced to the window.

Wet oak leaves pressed against the glass and slid down like slow green hands.

The big oak near the highway was tearing itself apart. Lightning must've hit it. One half of the huge tree crashed down behind the house. Dead branches snapped off it like crisp icicles. The other half slammed across the highway, blocking the crossroads with a barricade of branches.

Zack and Zipper pressed their noses against the window.

"Wow. Awesome."

Zack sensed movement. On the far side of the fallen tree.

He wasn't sure, but he thought he saw the shadow of a man walking through the woods. A man with a big swoop of combed-back hair.

"Zack?" his dad called from downstairs.

He turned to answer. "Yeah?"

"You guys okay?"

"Yeah. We're fine."

When he looked out the window again, the man was gone.

It feels good to be back inside a body—the same nineteen-year-old body he died in.

He still wears the boots, blue jeans, and black leather jacket he wore on the final night of his life. His hair is still full and thick, still combed straight back with a wavy doo-wop flip, still glued in place by glistening Brylcreem.

Wherever he goes, he leaves behind the minty scent of his oily hair cream.

He walks away from the oak tree and down to the road.

His flip-top Ford Thunderbird glimmers in the moonlight. The chrome grillwork on the convertible sparkles. There's no hint of where the front end crumpled and slammed the V-8 engine back into the driver's seat to crush his legs.

He hops in. Grips the steering wheel. Listens to the bent-eight engine purr and roar. He is ready to peel wheels and raise hell.

Raise some before he has to go there.

He had been terrified when the lightning bolt struck his tree, afraid it was God calling in the loan on his soul, demanding payment in full and interest past due.

When the tree split, he figured he was a goner, that it was time to move on, time to finally leave this limbo where he had been held prisoner for nearly fifty years.

But it seems he isn't heading downstairs for fire, brimstone, and pokes from the devil's pitchfork. Not just yet, anyway.

The stump. The roots. They sink deep into the earth. They hold him here. He doesn't have to let go or move on.

He glances up toward the second-story window of the house behind him.

The boy's bedroom.

I'll be back for you later, four-eyes. Never did like nerds who wore glasses. Counting the seconds between the lightning and the thunder? What a baby.

He has killed children before.

He looks forward to doing it again.

20

"That was pretty incredible, hunh?"

"Yeah."

"Zipper wasn't afraid when the tree came down?"

"Nah." Zipper was on top of Zack's bedspread, curled up against his legs. Zack was tucked in under the covers. "We're both fine, Dad."

"Good. I'll call those tree men first thing tomorrow. Get the backyard cleaned up."

"Cool."

"Good night, Zack."

His father flicked off the light. Closed the bedroom door.

Zack didn't dare mention the shadow man he had seen because his father would assume he was making up another story with what his mother used to call his over-active imagination. The way she said it? She meant Zack was a liar.

21

He has a fierce hunger for a cheeseburger, fries, and a thick chocolate shake.

But the Burger Barn is gone. Something called Chuck E. Cheese has taken its place.

He wants that cheeseburger bad. Hasn't had one in fifty years.

He jams the Thunderbird into reverse and peels wheels.

No one sees his car. No one hears it. They sense only a slight movement of wind, feel a cold swirl of air.

He makes a hard left turn and heads toward the river.

I'll go down to the factory, he thinks. *Follow somebody on lunch break. Find a cheeseburger.*

He has no concept of time. It is four a.m. Nobody will be going to lunch, especially no employees of the Spratling Clockworks Factory, which shuttered its doors in 1983.

He pulls into a crumbling parking lot outside an enormous redbrick building—an empty shell three stories tall with arched windows. The giant Spratling Stands the Test of Time sign is rusty and faded.

He had started working for Julius Spratling in 1951. He pushed a broom, cleaned up trash, and flirted with the factory girls—many of whom he took out back to his secret love nest.

The machine shop. It was his passion pit—even after he was married.

In the east, the sun begins to rise. Somehow he understands he has to leave. When dawn comes, he'll be gone. But he knows he will return come nightfall. He senses it.

He has work to do, unfinished business.

He also has time.

If that lightning bolt couldn't send me to hell, what on earth can?

22

"We'll chop it up into firewood, mulch the crown."

Tony Mandica had brought a crew of six tree men with him to the Jennings house early Saturday morning.

"Would you guys like some coffee?" Judy asked.

"You got a bathroom we can use later?"

"Uh, sure. Right off the kitchen."

"In that case, pour me a big 'un!"

Judy smiled. Poured coffee into paper cups. Four of the new home's five bathrooms were still operational. The one off Zack's bedroom was a mess. Good thing the plumber was coming that afternoon, too.

"Is your father here?" Judy asked Mandica.

"Yeah. Probably someplace shady taking a nap. I swear, if his name wasn't already on the truck, I'd fire him!"

"Do you think he'd like some coffee?"

"Never saw him turn down a free cup."

"Zack? Can you and Zipper take Mr. Mandica some coffee?"

Zack really didn't want to traipse around in the evil trees looking for an old man napping like Rip van Winkle.

But Judy gave him that smile. What else could he do? Tell her he was afraid?

"Sure," he said.

He took the coffee and headed into the woods. Zipper followed him.

Zack saw the old man sitting on a big rock staring at the jagged stump left when the oak toppled over. He had a chain saw sitting near his feet, but it wasn't running.

Zipper barked and the old man looked up.

"I brought you some coffee, sir."

The old man's eyes looked as milky as bug guts.

"I tried to bring this tree down once before." The old man pointed at a cluster of angry gashes scarring the bark. "See there? That's where I took my ax to it. Took a saw to it, too. Bent my ax head. Chewed up my saw blade."

The old man didn't look at Zack and wasn't actually talking to him, either. He was saying stuff to the empty air and Zack just happened to be the only person close enough to hear it.

"When they come to me, I told 'em I'd chop it down. But I couldn't 'cause it's a devil tree."

The old man wiped at his mouth with the sleeve of his flannel shirt. The temperature was way over eighty degrees, but he was wearing red-checked flannel.

Because the old man is crazy.

"They wouldn't let me be. *Chop it down, chop it down, chop it down.* Every night, they'd come at me in my dreams. *Chop it down, chop it down, chop it down.*"

Zack placed the coffee cup on the ground.

"I'll leave your coffee. . . ."

The old man spun around. Glared at Zack.

"It's a devil tree, boy! You hear me? The gateway to hell! That's why you never see no snow around it come winter. Hell's too hot. Melts the snow outside its back door!"

"I think I hear my father calling."

"God himself had to bring this tree down," the old man ranted, "because no mortal man could!"

"Okay. So long, sir."

Zack ran the hundred-yard dash back to his house as fast as he could. Zipper ran after him.

Great. The oak tree wasn't just evil; it was hell's back door.

Now Zack had something else not to tell anyone.

23

While the tree crew worked on the felled tree, Zack walked up Stonebriar Road with his father, who had decided this was the perfect Saturday to go see if any other kids were living in the neighborhood.

They walked past several houses still under construction.

"When I was a boy, a bunch of us hung out together all summer long. We gave each other nicknames: Cowboy, Moose, Stinky. He, you know, didn't shower much."

"What'd they call you?"

"Ratfink."

"Really? Why?"

"Because my father was the sheriff. The other guys were afraid I'd rat them out if we ever did anything bad."

"Did you?"

"Nope. It's against the guy code. A guy never rats out his buddies unless, you know, uh, one of their fathers needs to know something important. A guy always tells his dad everything important. That's another part of the same code. . . ."

"But your dad was the sheriff. So that part of the code sort of violates the first part."

"Yeah." Zack's father was having trouble wiggling out of that one, so he changed the subject. "Hey, there's a couple guys!"

Zack saw four boys his age tossing a baseball around in an empty lot.

"Maybe they're getting up a game," his dad said eagerly.

A tough-looking boy stood in the center of the others. He pounded a ball into his mitt and glared at Zack. Toughie smirked, then snorted. Zack knew what that meant: Another bully already hated his geeky guts.

"You guys need another player?" Zack's father asked.

"Not really," said the tough guy.

"Okay," said Zack. "We'd better go home, Dad."

Zipper barked in agreement.

"Just a minute," his father said. "Boys, I'm George Jennings. We just moved in—down the street. The Victorian there."

"What's a Victorian?"

"A famous style of architecture."

Another snort from Tough Stuff. "Looks like a doll-house."

"That's right. Most dollhouses are fashioned after Victorian homes. What's your name, son?"

"Kyle. Kyle Snertz."

"Do you live around here?"

"Duh."

Zack's father chose to ignore Snertz's sarcasm.

"This is my son, Zack. Zack? Say hi to Kyle."

"Hey," Zack mumbled.

Kyle Snertz snorted back some more wet stuff. The guy seemed to have a ton of snot stuck inside his nose.

"Say, guess what?" Zack's father said to Kyle.

"What?"

"We're going to build a tree fort!"

"We are?" The news flash surprised Zack.

Kyle was suddenly interested. "Cool. You gonna steal wood and junk from the construction sites?"

"No." Zack's father chuckled. "We're not going to *steal* anything. I thought we'd run out to Home Depot. You guys are welcome to come along with us if you'd like." The cell phone clipped to his belt started chirping. "Excuse me, fellas." He walked away to take the call.

The other boys moved in behind Kyle. Zack could tell he was their leader. The alpha dog.

"So, four-eyes," Kyle sneered low so Zack's dad couldn't hear. "You live in a dollhouse?"

Zack didn't answer. Kyle was big. The boys who wanted to beat him up usually were. Big and moist.

Kyle moved closer. Close enough that Zack could smell his sweat and know it stank like rancid chicken soup. "Seeing how you live in a dollhouse, maybe we should call you Barbie from now on."

Great. A nickname. Like Stinky or Ratfink, only worse.

"My name is Zack." He mumbled it to the dirt.

"No, it's not, *Barbie.*"

Zipper snapped at the boy's ankle.

"Hey! If your stupid dog bites me, I swear I'll sue!" Kyle used both hands to smack Zack hard in the chest.

"Hey, hey, hey." Zack's dad saw the shove, closed up his cell. "What seems to be the problem?"

"Stupid dog tried to bite me."

"Whoa," said Zack's father. "Take it easy there, Kyle."

"Ahhhhh, bite me, old man."

"What?"

"I said, 'Bite me, old man.' What's the matter? You deaf?"

"Okay. I'm going to have a word with your parents. Where exactly do you live?"

"That's for me to know and you to find out!"

"Dad?" Zack tugged at his father's arm. "Let's go home."

Kyle Snertz spat on the ground. Zack knew what it meant: "Don't come back unless you want trouble."

"So who called?" Zack asked when they were a couple hundred feet up the street.

"Work. About my business trip next week."

"Malaysia?"

"Yeah."

"Cool."

"Hey, Barbie," Kyle Snertz yelled after them. "Have fun in your *tree fort*!"

The way Snertz said "tree fort" made it sound like the sissiest thing any boy could ever do.

It also made Zack wish he could fly away to Malaysia with his father.

Either Malaysia or Timbuktu.

As the sun goes down, he sees an old man sitting on the stump of what used to be his tree.

He doesn't wish to be seen, so he isn't.

He would like to kill the geezer who long ago tried to chop down his tree. But he can't. He can't do much besides make noise and, if he tries real hard, rattle things.

Now something draws him toward the house. Something strong. He drifts out of the trees.

No one sees him because he doesn't wish to be seen.

Not just yet, anyway.

The plumber had never seen such a mess in a bathroom.

He uncoiled his motorized snake and worked the long, flexible wire down into the toilet. He flipped the power switch and the steel cable rooted its way farther down the drain. It spun and ground and churned. A minute later, he felt the far end hit something. The clog.

"Bingo! Got it!"

The cable cut through whatever wad of muck was blocking the sewer line, and the toilet bowl sucked itself dry.

That's when the plumber smelled something. Not sewer gas. Something oily and minty.

Like Brylcreem. Billy had tried that goop once. When he was a kid, Mee Maw had slicked down his hair with the stuff on the day he'd posed for his sixth-grade class picture, the same day his name went from Billy O'Claire to Billy O'Greasy Hair.

He'd never forget that smell—like someone had rubbed his head with a peppermint stick made out of Crisco.

All of a sudden, Billy had an incredible craving for a big juicy burger. Plus a side of fries. And a chocolate milk shake. Maybe two or three of each.

Billy dropped his sewer rooter with a *clunk* and a *thud* on the tile floor. He didn't bother packing up his wrenches. He'd come back later for his tools.

Right now he *had* to have a hamburger.

He walked out of the bathroom like a zombie. A very hungry, burger-crazed zombie.

And then—just as suddenly—the urge passed.

Good, he thought. *I've always been more of a nachos kind of guy.*

"You ought to grind down the stump," the tree man suggested to Judy.

It was after dusk, but the big oak was finally chipped and mulched.

"Grinding costs extra, but I've got this machine that'll chew right through it."

"No," Judy said gently.

"All right. How about we dig it out? We bring in a backhoe and—"

"No. We should save the stump. It'll give Miss Spratling someplace to hang her *descanso*."

"Des-what-so?"

"It's a Spanish word. Means 'memorial.' "

"All right. Suit yourself. But if you change your mind, give me a call."

"Okay," said Judy. "Zack?"

"Yeah?"

"Can you nail everything back up? Hang the cross and flower bucket on the highway side of the stump?"

"Now?"

"No, honey. It's dark. Let's do it tomorrow."

"Yeah," Mandica said. "You're right. We should all knock off for the night." Mandica looked around the backyard. "Anybody seen Pop?"

A chain saw roared to life out in the woods.

I know, I know. I heard you the first time. I heard all of you!"

The old man was shouting at the darkness between two birch trees. His thrumming chain saw hung limply alongside his leg. Its sharp teeth rattled and chugged and slid around the tip of the blade.

"If I finish the job, will you leave me be?"

No one answered because no one was there.

The old man goosed the saw's throttle. The throaty engine rumbled and roared. He pressed its spinning teeth against the jagged wood.

Sparks flew as if he were trying to slice into a steel I beam.

27

He drifts back to what is left of his tree.

The burger will have to wait because he sees what the old man is trying to do. Sees him attacking the stump with a chittering chain saw. Sees red sparks and chunks of wood flying from the snaggletoothed stump.

He knows he can't stop the old man.

But it is dark now, so he can show himself.

He does.

28

Sweat pouring down his face, the old man finally cut a smooth edge across the top of the stump.

"Pop?"

He could hear his son off in the distance, near the house, but didn't answer.

A young man in blue jeans and a leather jacket appeared in the small clearing near the stump. A man with slicked-back hair. Pasty flesh. Cold and evil eyes. "What do you think you're doing?"

The old man dropped his chain saw and clutched his chest. Tried to breathe. The saw's razor-sharp blade chewed through the toe of his work boot.

Mr. Mandica toppled sideways.

Clint Eberhart laughed and vanished into the soft night air.

The next day, Zack and Zipper went out into the woods ringing the backyard to check out the stump.

Judy said maintaining the memorial was even more important now that Mr. Mandica had died so close to the old tree. So Zack had a claw hammer looped through his belt and a pocketful of nails scratching against his thigh as he set off to make the repairs.

"There's nothing to be afraid of," he said to Zipper. "I don't think the Wicked Witch will be back here today. Not on a Sunday."

Zack examined the stump. It was gigantic. At least ten feet across. The ground around it had heaved up some, but the rooted base was still intact. Zack saw the white cross and rusty bucket lying on the ground.

"Come on. We'd better fix it."

While Zack hammered, he studied the depression

Mr. Mandica's body had made in the damp dirt when he died. It looked exactly like the indentation his mother had left in her hospital-bed mattress.

Zack straightened the cross and pushed a new nail through an old hole near its top. Next he nailed in the bucket.

"Okay. Where are the stupid flowers?"

Zack looked around on the ground.

"Make ready the way of the Lord!" cried a stern voice behind him.

Zack spun around and saw an angry man in a sweltering black suit. The man was tall and pencil thin and wore a black hat the size and shape of a pizza pan. Some sleepy-eyed kids stood behind him in single-file lines. They looked miserable.

"Why dost thou undo what the Lord hath done?" the man shouted. He held a black book with colored ribbons streaming out from gold-edged pages. A Bible.

The children behind the man looked weird. The boys all wore identical short-sleeve shirts. The girls had on dresses that swung out like bells. The boys had buzz cuts. The girls, pigtails. All their lips were tiny O's—like they breathed only through their mouths or were posing to be Pilgrim candles for Thanksgiving.

"Heed my words! Clear away this stump!"

"Howdy, folks!" someone yelled from off to the right.

Zack spied a boy about his own age dressed in bib

overalls but with no shirt on underneath the shoulder straps. The boy was barefoot and held a slingshot aimed at the man in black. He let loose a small stone that whacked the skinny man in his shin.

"Gotcha!"

Zipper wagged his tail. He liked this boy with the slingshot.

The man in the pizza hat shook his fist. "Scallywag!"

"Sir, I think it's time you and the kiddies headed back to camp. So make like a tree and leaf."

Zack smiled. Nodded at the boy.

"Galdern Bible campers," the boy said, shaking his head.

"Yeah." Zack acted like he knew what the boy was talking about. He turned back to face the man in black.

But he was gone. So were the children.

"Where'd they all go?"

"Back to where they come from, I reckon." The boy tucked his slingshot into the front flap of his overalls. "I'm Davy. Davy Wilcox."

"I'm Zack. Zack Jennings."

"Pleased to meet ya. Where d'ya live?"

"Right here."

"The new house?"

"Yep."

"Swell!"

"You live around here?"

"Sure do. Moved up from Kentucky a few years back."

That explained why he talked so funny.

"We're right across the highway. See? On the farm over yonder."

Zack looked across the highway and saw patches of a brown field filled with dead cornstalks.

"That's our field. We keep the cows out back."

"In the barn?" Zack asked.

"That's right. You ever work on a farm, Zack?"

"No. But I had this Old McDonald farm set once."

"With plastic animals and such like that?"

"Yeah," Zack said, immediately wondering why he felt compelled to tell this boy about his baby toys.

Tell him about your G.I. Joes, too, why don't you? Then he can make fun of you for playing with dolls just like all your other new neighbors.

"I had me one of them toy farm sets, too," Davy said. "I thought it was all kinds of swell. Did you have the tractor?"

"Yeah. I chased the cows with it."

"Hey, that sounds neat. Chasing cows with a tractor? Sounds real neat. So you and your folks just moved in?"

"Yep. Last Monday."

"Swell. Not many cool kids live around here. Just a couple jerks. Didja meet Kyle Snertz yet?"

"Yeah. Kind of."

"What a dipstick. He can't play baseball, neither. Swings that bat like a galdern girl."

"Really?"

"Does he ever!"

Davy flung his arms around in crazy circles like a blindfolded baboon swatting at a piñata.

"He's all show and no blow!"

"He doesn't scare you?"

"Snotty Snertz? Heck no."

Zack spun around in circles, imitating Davy Wilcox imitating Snertz. Zipper sprang up on his hind legs and spun around in circles, too.

When they saw that, the two boys started laughing.

"Dang! Even your dog swings better than Snertz!"

Zack laughed even harder and realized he might've just found his first real friend.

30

That night, Clint Eberhart sought out the plumber.

The one to do all the things I can't do myself.

Eberhart was slowly adjusting to his new "condition." By day, he was vapor invisible to all except children with very vivid imaginations. By night, he could freely roam the earth in his former body and car. But in both instances his physical abilities were severely limited.

In fact, he couldn't do anything.

He couldn't eat.

He couldn't fight.

All he could do was materialize, prowl in the shadows, and make noises.

Of course, at night he could scare the pants off just about anybody. Why, he could give an old man with a chain saw a heart attack if he timed his fade-in just so.

But if he wanted to take care of any unfinished business, Clint Eberhart would need a good pair of human hands.

So he picked the plumber.

The pickup truck was parked on the soft shoulder of the highway near the crossroads.

Billy O'Claire sat up front, staring at the blinking red light. Listening to the crickets. Swatting the mosquitoes nibbling at his neck. After a solid smack and a squish, he checked his watch.

It was almost exactly the same time as it had been that night when he'd seen the motorcycle cop standing in the crossroads. Billy took a sip from a two-liter bottle of soda. He wanted to be wide awake when the mystery man reappeared.

He knotted his eyes and stared straight ahead. "I double-dog dare you to show your face again!"

Well, not his face. He hadn't really shown it that first time, since the cop didn't *have* a face. Billy wondered how he kept his sunglasses in place without a nose for them to sit on. He also wondered why he wore sunglasses in the middle of the night.

Somebody pulled in behind Billy.

He turned around, looked out his rear window. He didn't see any headlights, but he could make out the shadowy silhouette of a wide-bodied convertible. None of his friends drove classic convertibles with tail fins.

Goose bumps exploded on his arms. It felt like some-body was outside his truck looking in.

Slowly, barely moving, Billy turned to his left.

A man with slicked-back black hair was staring at him. Grinning.

"Hey there," the man said, his voice raw and raspy.

"Who are you?" Billy asked.

"Someone just passing through."

Billy looked into the guy's eyes. Man—they were so blue. Like the plates at the diner.

"So, plumber—what's your name?"

"Billy."

"Billy what?"

"O'Claire."

That seemed to startle the man.

"You from around here?" he asked.

"Lived here my whole life."

"And you say you're an O'Claire?"

"Been one of those my whole life, too."

"What's your father's name?"

"Tommy O'Claire."

"Never heard of him."

"He died a long time ago. Maybe you know my Mee Maw."

"Your what?"

"My grandmother. Mary O'Claire."

Now the strange dude looked angry.

"Mary O'Claire? Is her family from up near Spencer?"

"I don't know. I could ask her, I guess."

"She's alive? She didn't die in 1958?"

Billy laughed. "Well, uh, no—I don't think so. I just saw her the other day and she didn't look dead."

The man with the plastered-back hair leaned closer to the door.

"You're a wisenheimer, hunh?"

"A what?"

"Where can I find her? Where's young Mary O'Claire hiding?"

"Young?" This guy was cracking Billy up. "I told you, dude—she's my *grandmother*. She lives in the old folks home. Guess what? That means she's *old*."

The guy made the pupils floating inside his eyes go wider, turned them into hypnotic sinkholes. Billy felt drowsy, like he needed to take a nap.

He felt like a burger-craving zombie again.

A zombie who would do anything this guy asked him to.

Anything at all.

31

"So what do you want to do today, sweetie?"

On Monday morning, Judy and Zack ate cereal in the breakfast nook. His father had left for the train station and the commute to his law firm in New York City long before either one of them was awake. It was their first morning alone together in the big house. They were sticking to cold breakfast foods. Judy had almost started another fire using aluminum foil in the microwave.

"Nothing," Zack said, slurping his cereal. "Probably just, you know, hang out with Davy."

"Who's Davy?"

"This guy I met."

"Really? Does he live around here?"

"Yep. Right across the highway. On the farm."

"Have fun, but be careful, okay?"

"We will."

Judy tried to remember all the things her mother used to say when she went outside to play.

"Look both ways if you cross the street. Don't run around with scissors. And . . ."

"I won't take any candy from strangers."

"Good. I knew I forgot one."

"So Judy's your stepmother, hunh?" Davy asked while Zack hammered a two-by-four into the tree.

They had decided to go ahead and build a tree house. Zack had found a few boards piled up in the garage—wood left over from when the house was built.

"Yeah," Zack said, "she's kind of new at it and all. But she's not wicked or anything. Not like the stepmothers in Disney cartoons."

"Well, that's good," Davy said. "Where's your real mom?"

"Dead."

"Sorry, pardner. I didn't know. I just figured your folks got divorced or what have you."

"She had cancer. Smoked too many cigarettes."

"Dang coffin nails. Reckon you miss her, hunh?"

"I guess," Zack said, but then he realized that maybe he could tell Davy the truth. "Well, actually, I don't really miss her all that much."

"Is that so?"

Zack shrugged. "My mother never really liked me."

"I see."

"She used to say I ruined her life."

"Dang."

"That's why she always wanted to run away from home. Sometimes she would, too. She'd rent a room in a hotel and disappear for a couple days. And when she was home? She'd stay in bed until three or four in the afternoon. I'd come home from school and she'd still be sleeping. If I woke her up, she'd just tell me to leave her alone and light another cigarette because I was driving her crazy."

"Sounds like a dern sad lady."

"I guess. I didn't mean to mess her up like I did."

"Zack?"

"Yeah?"

"I ain't no Seigfried Freud, but I don't reckon you're the one what messed her up."

"No?"

"No, sir. I reckon she got that way long before you came along. You got enough nails there, pardner?"

"Yep." Zack stuck a nail in his mouth and held it between his lips, just like he had seen a carpenter do on TV once. He was glad he'd told Davy the truth. It felt good to finally have a friend, somebody he could actually talk with.

"Ladder's lookin' galdern good," Davy said.

"Unh-hunh."

"I figure we oughta work our way up to that crook

there," Davy said, placing his hands on his hips and studying the tree. "Then we should start laying in some floorboards."

"Unh-hunh," Zack said, concentrating on his hammering. "We'll need more wood."

"My pops said we could take all we need from out behind the barn."

"Cool!"

"Uh-oh," Davy said. "Cheese it. Looks like we got company."

Zack saw a big black Cadillac pull off the highway.

"It's her!"

"Who?"

"The old lady!" Zack whispered. "The Wicked Witch I told you about."

Zipper grumbled softly.

"Quick!" said Davy. "Over there! We can hide behind them sticker bushes and spy on her! We'll be like Davy Crockett scoutin' out the Injuns!"

"Okay," Zack said.

Hanging out with Davy was fun.

Even when it was sort of scary, it was still fun.

32

Gerda Spratling had not seen her roadside memorial since the thunderstorm.

"Dear God in heaven!" She scrabbled up the path into the forest.

"Mr. Willoughby?"

"Yes, ma'am?"

"Call the police! Call them now!"

"The police, Miss Spratling?"

"Some vandal has chopped down my tree!"

"Is something wrong?" Judy came into the clearing near the stump. She had been in the backyard gardening when she heard an old lady screaming for the police. "Are you all right?"

"The tree!" Miss Spratling gasped. "What goes on here?"

"Lightning."

"What?"

"The tree was hit by lightning."

"Impossible."

"No, not really. Sure, the odds are like a billion to one, but every now and then the lightning gets lucky."

"What? How dare you make fun of my memorial!"

Judy realized who the woman had to be and felt terrible.

"Um—are you Gerda Spratling?"

Miss Spratling fell to her knees.

"I am *so* sorry," said Judy.

The elderly lady stretched out her trembling arms and tried to wrap them around the stump.

"We just moved in last week and . . ."

The old woman wailed.

"We found the cross and flower bucket. . . ."

She wailed louder.

"I was going to plant some flowers back here. Make a memorial garden."

The wailing stopped.

"You were?" Miss Spratling sniffled back a tear.

"Yes."

Of course Judy was lying, but she had to say something or the old lady kneeling in the dirt might give herself a heart attack, and one heart attack a week was enough for any backyard.

"I thought a small garden might make up for the terrible loss of your tree."

The old lady's face softened. Her head tilted down toward her shoulder.

"How very kind of you, dear."

Judy knelt beside the stump and started digging a hole between two huge roots.

"A memorial garden will make Clint's shrine even more glorious!" said Miss Spratling. "They ran him off the road, you know."

"Really?" Judy scooped out more dirt.

"Oh, yes. June 21, 1958. I will never forget." Miss Spratling stood and dusted leaf crumbs off her black dress. "You're very kind to do this for Clint. What's your name, dear?"

"Judy. Judy Magruder. Or you can call me Judy Jennings. I'm a newlywed."

"Is that so?"

"Yes, ma'am. I just married George Jennings. His father used to be the sheriff up here."

Judy was too busy planting the flowers to see the old lady's smile curl down into a frown.

"Really? My, my, my. Judy *Jennings*? What a lovely, lovely name."

Zack, Davy, and Zipper tromped through the corn-field on the far side of the highway.

The sun had bleached the dead stalks to a watery shade of brown. As they slogged across the muddy field, Zack's socks squished.

"How much farther?"

"Well, pardner, the lumber pile's clear up yonder. Out behind the barn. Sure is a swell day for a hike, though, ain't it?"

The air was thick, bugs were buzzing around his ankles and his eyes, the smell of rotten cornstalks baking in the sun was everywhere, and Zack couldn't even see a barn.

Just swell.

"Don't this dang meadow smell sweet?"

"I guess," Zack said. He thought Davy had a funny way of talking.

Must come from growing up on a farm or coming from Kentucky.

But Zack didn't mind. He liked Davy, even when he used weird words like "swell" and "keen." Or when he called him "pardner" or "sport." Sure beat being "Barbie."

"Maybe we ought to skirt up there alongside the road. Stick to the shade under them trees."

"Good idea," said Zack, slapping at some kind of bug burrowing into his ear.

"I figure if we can lay in the tree house floor this afternoon, we'll be off to a swell start," said Davy as they trekked through the trees. "We'll build us a regular crow's nest. Just like a pack of pirates!"

"Yeah! We can make people walk the plank and stuff!"

"Sure. It'll be swell!"

They stepped into a sunny spot.

A man blocked their path.

A businessman dressed in a brown suit with a white handkerchief tucked into the breast pocket. He was wearing a hat like Zack had seen in old movies. A fedora, they called it.

"Hey there, fellers!" The businessman leaned into the sunlight. "Off on a scavenger hunt?" There was a boxy sample case sitting on the ground near his shiny shoes. He carried a raincoat tucked under his arm—even though there wasn't a single cloud in the sky.

"I heard you two are building a tree fort!" said the businessman. "Well, boys, I'm the top aluminum-siding salesman in these parts. Clarence W. Billings is my name and—"

"We don't need no galdern aluminum siding," said Davy.

"We're just building a tree house," added Zack.

"So leave us be, tin man!"

"Easy, son. Easy. What if I told you fellers you don't have to hike across the highway all the livelong day to fetch your lumber?"

"What do you mean?" Davy put his hands on his hips.

"Well, son, I couldn't help but notice all the building supplies stacked on the other side of the road at those construction sites."

"So?"

"Well, son, those are what we in the construction trade call scrap piles. Feller can help himself to all the scrap he wants. All the boards and plywood out front of those brand-new bungalows? That's yours and free for the taking."

Davy was intrigued. "Is that so?"

"Darn tootin'," said the salesman.

Zack scratched a fresh mosquito bite behind his knee. "Might save us a lot of marching through the mud, Davy."

"You're right there, pardner."

The aluminum-siding salesman rocked gently on his heels, widened his smile.

Davy nodded at the businessman. "Well, sir, I reckon you ain't a bad egg after all."

"Just trying to lend a hand, son." The salesman tipped his hat. "Say, now, I wonder if you two fellers might do *me* a little favor. Make everything square between us?"

"What kind of favor?" Davy asked.

Zack's heart beat faster. This stranger could be one of those men his father warned him about. The ones who wanted you to climb into their cars.

"Tell me, boys: Have you seen that dag-blasted stump over on the other side of the road?"

"Sure," said Davy.

"Well, we already talked to this one feller about taking it out, but he couldn't finish the job. Had him a heart attack. But you boys—well, you're young and strong and I bet you could figure out a way to rip that stump right out of the ground! Yes, sir, I wager—"

"Run for it, Zack!" Davy yelled.

Zack, Davy, and Zipper tore through the trees. They ran down the embankment, crossed the highway, and made it to the far side of the road.

"See you later, alligator!" Davy shouted with a laugh.

"Boys?" Billings called after them.

But the boys were gone.

"Encouraging children to steal, Mr. Billings? Tsk, tsk, tsk."

The businessman turned and saw a nun standing next to him. She carried a small traveling valise.

"Desperate times call for desperate measures, Sister."

"Stealing is a sin."

"But . . ."

"Do not despair. That boy is the chosen one."

"You sure about that? He looks kind of puny. Glasses are awful thick, too."

"He will do what needs to be done," the nun said serenely. "Zachary Jennings will not let us down."

Zack and Davy sat with their legs dangling over the edge of their tree platform.

Zack had just nailed down a sheet of plywood they had found in one of the scrap piles up Stonebriar Road. Since the floor of their tree house was only ten feet high, Zack had been able to carry Zipper up with him.

"We should build Zipper an elevator," Davy suggested.

"How?"

"Rig up a bucket on a rope. Loop it off that branch."

"Hey, cool. Great idea."

Zipper barked his approval of the plan.

It was close to six p.m. The first day of work was finished. Zack had never felt so good about anything in his life.

"This is awesome," he said, taking in the view.

"I'll say. Why, you can see just about everything from up here!"

"Yep."

"Yes, sir," Davy sighed. "You can even see the stuff you wish you couldn't."

"What do you mean?"

Davy gestured at Judy's freshly planted flowers circling the ten-foot-wide stump.

" 'Ring around the rosies, a pocketful of posies,' " said Davy. "Kind of ruins everything."

"Really?"

"Frilly little flowers? Docked so dadgum close to our pirate ship? Shoot, anybody driving by will think this is some kind of *girl's* tree house."

"Wow. I never thought about it that way."

"Me neither. Not till we climbed on up. But it just sort of hits you right between the peepers when you're perched here, don't it?"

"Yeah," Zack said. "I guess so."

"And that white wooden cross? That makes it look like we're back here playing Bible camp! Jiminy Christmas, I wish we could just tear it down, pull up the flowers, and rip that dadgum stump clear out of the ground. The whole thing razzes my berries."

"Yeah," Zack said. "Razzes my berries, too."

"That Mr. Billings feller was right. We need to get rid of it."

"Yeah," Zack agreed. "But how?"

Billy O'Claire sat in a booth choking down his third double cheeseburger.

The burgers were juicy and the first two had been okay, especially with a large side of fries. The third, however, tasted like what it was: about a half pound of cooked cow.

Billy belched. "Oh, man."

His stomach hurt. He'd also inhaled three chocolate shakes in less than fifteen minutes.

"*Finish my burger!*" said a nagging voice inside his head. "*I haven't had one in fifty years!*"

Billy took another weary bite. Tried to mash the meat and bread around in his mouth. It was becoming more of a chore with every chew.

He had never been much of a burger guy before. He was more into pizza. Nachos. Buffalo wings.

But it had been nothing but cheeseburgers, fries, and milk shakes since he had met the guy with the slicked-back hair.

Billy still didn't know why the guy kept showing up. He just knew he'd be back soon because tonight was the night he wanted to meet Billy's grandmother: Mary O'Claire.

36

Zack's father didn't come home until nine p.m. on Monday, his first day commuting to his office in the city.

Judy propped open the lid on a cardboard pizza box. "Sorry it's cold."

"I'm sorry I had to work so late. It's this meeting next week in Malaysia."

"Well," said Judy, "if you're traveling halfway around the world, it's probably smart to do your homework before you leave home."

"Guess how long I'll be on airplanes?"

"As long as you'll be in Malaysia?"

"Close. The meeting lasts two days. The flight takes nineteen hours—each way."

"Ouch. Better pack a good book."

"I think I'd better pack the whole library."

Zack sat on his stool, hoping his father and Judy

wouldn't start yelling at each other like his father and his real mother always used to do whenever his father worked late. Those arguments would start over long hours at the office and eventually lead back to Zack.

"You're the one who wanted children!" his mother would scream. In fact, his mother had managed to work that particular line into any argument, no matter what it was about: "You don't like how I spend money? Fine! You're the one who wanted children!"

Zack worried that Judy might start feeling the same way. She might end up hating Zack because she was the one stuck in Connecticut taking care of him and he wasn't even her real kid!

He had to do something. Fast. He had to change the subject before the newlyweds tumbled into their first argument and figured out who the real problem was: Him!

"We started building a tree house today!" he blurted out. "Me and Davy."

Judy and his father stared at him.

"Who's Davy?" his father asked.

"A neat guy who lives on a farm across the highway."

"Can't wait to meet him," his father said, balancing a limp piece of soggy pizza.

"Me too," Judy added.

Zipper crawled out from under the table, sat back on his haunches, and raised his front paws.

"Hmmm," said Zack's father, "looks like somebody

else around here likes cold pizza. You know, in law school, we used to eat cold pizza for breakfast and—"

"What was that?" said Judy. "Did you see that?"

"What?" Zack climbed off his stool.

"I saw a light. It went swinging by the window."

"Could be a car," George said, his mouth full of chewy cheese. "Down on the highway with its headlights aimed wrong." He peeled off a pepperoni and presented it to Zipper, who wasn't interested anymore. The dog scampered over to the window.

"There it is!" Judy said. "See? In the trees? Looks like a flashlight. Come on—let's go investigate."

"Might be dangerous," said Zack.

"Might be fun!" his father said. "C'mon, Zack. Bring Zipper. He'll protect us." He got up and pulled a flashlight out of its recharging cradle near the back door. Judy grabbed her jean jacket. Zipper barked.

Zack had no choice.

He had to journey once again into the evil woods fringing his backyard. And this time, he'd have to do it in the dark.

Great.

But then he realized something: This time, he wouldn't be alone. This time, his whole family was coming with him.

"You're right, Dad. Let's go see who's out there!"

37

"My guess is a lost cat," Zack's father said as they made their way across the backyard. "Probably heard Curiosity Cat moved in next door."

"It's probably just somebody playing with a flashlight," said Judy.

"Nah. Too bright for a flashlight," said Zack's father. "I'm figuring it's a train that ran off the tracks and is making all local stops."

The beam hit them like the searchlight in a prison movie.

"Don't shoot!" Zack's dad said dramatically, and held up his hands. "We surrender!"

"That the boy?" asked a voice from behind the unbelievably bright light.

"That's him, Pops. Hey, Zack!"

"Hey, Davy," Zack said. Zipper wagged his tail.

"These your folks?"

"Yep. My dad and my stepmom."

"Hiya, folks," Davy said. "Sorry if we gave you a scare. Wanted my pops to take a gander at our tree house."

The light lowered. A rail-thin farmer stood next to Davy. He wore a tattered Huck Finn straw hat with salty white sweat ringing its crown.

"Howdy," the farmer said.

"Hi. I'm George Jennings. This is my wife, Judy. My son, Zack. And, of course, Zipper."

Zipper wagged his tail.

"That's my pops," said Davy. "He don't talk much. Right, Pops?"

"Yep."

"But he sure wanted to see what we built up in the tree today."

"Me too." Zack's dad aimed his flashlight at the crooked boards and uneven floor. "That it?"

"Sure is, Mr. Jennings. Ain't she something?"

"That's our pirate ship!" Zack said. "See? There's the ladder like you have to climb to get to the crow's nest."

Zack's father nodded. "Very nice."

"Davy, would you and your father like some ice cream?" Judy asked. "I could put on a pot of coffee."

"No thanks, ma'am. We need to head on back. Pops just wanted to meet my new buddy, Zack."

"Yep."

"Well, it was very nice to meet you both," said Judy.

"It was swell meeting you, too, Mrs. J. Zack sure is lucky to have such a nice new mom. Pretty as a galdern picture postcard, too."

"Well, aren't you the little charmer?"

"No, ma'am. I just call 'em like I see 'em. See you tomorrow, Zack!"

The old farmer nodded and touched his straw hat to say "So long." He and Davy disappeared into the shadows.

"Nice boy," Zack's father said.

"Sure is," said Zack.

"Do all the kids up here talk that way?"

"Nope. Just Davy. He's a farmer. And he was born in Kentucky."

"Oh. I see."

"I'm glad I met him," Judy said, draping an arm across Zack's shoulder. "He seems like a great guy."

"He is. Oh—guess what? He told me he *loves* cherry Kool-Aid."

"Really?"

"Yep."

"I was a grape man myself," Zack's dad said as he rested his hand on Zack's other shoulder. "Used to pour the powder on my tongue straight from the pouch!"

"Well," said Judy, "I haven't had any kind of galdern Kool-Aid in ages, but maybe I could pick some up at the galdern store."

"That would be swell," said Zack. "Just swell."

38

"Oh, Daddy! The son has come home!"

Gerda Spratling tottered around her bed in the mansion's library.

Mondays were always difficult. This, however, was the worst Monday ever. Today she had learned that the loathsome sheriff's son had come home to haunt her.

Miss Spratling's life had ended when her fiancé, Clint Eberhart, was killed in the crossroads. It ended again twenty-five years later when her father committed suicide. Death surrounded Gerda Spratling. Her whole life was nothing now but a long, slow crawl toward the grave, where she prayed she would be reunited with the two men she had lost.

Memories and anger. That was all she had left, all that dragged her out of bed every morning.

But George Jennings? He must be so happy. Married to

that pretty young thing with the flowers. Moving into a handsome new home.

She stared up at the highest bookshelf, at the rolling ladder, up to where her father had hanged himself.

"Sheriff Jennings made you do it, Daddy! I know he did!" She lurched across the room toward the ladder and wrapped one bony hand around a rung to hoist herself up.

"Daddy? Can you hear me? Daddy?"

Her foot slipped. She banged her chin against the sharp edge of a step. Warm blood trickled where she had bitten into her lip.

"Miss Spratling?"

Sharon rushed into the room and saw Miss Spratling sprawled out on the floor. "Let's get you up from there, ma'am."

"Get your hands off me, girl! Bring me my book!"

Sharon found the antique Bible on the bedside table and handed it to Miss Spratling. The old woman pried open the cracked leather cover and quickly located her most cherished passage.

Exodus. Chapter thirty-four. Verse seven.

The only words in the whole Bible that gave her any comfort:

"He does not leave the guilty unpunished; He punishes the children and their children for the sin of the fathers to the third and fourth generation."

To the third and fourth generation.

That meant God would punish the son for what his father, the sheriff, had done. God would also punish the *son's son*, the little brat with the filthy dog.

Miss Spratling only prayed that God would let her help.

39

Billy pulled his pickup truck into the parking lot of the old folks' home a little before midnight.

The guy with the slicked-back hair wasn't with him. He didn't cruise along behind Billy's truck in the phantom Thunderbird. He didn't even show himself.

He didn't have to do any of that anymore.

He and Billy had become one. Some kind of transference had taken place, and Clint Eberhart's soul was able to slide into Billy's body to take full control of everything the plumber said or did.

Billy stepped out of his truck and made his way to the bushes outside his grandmother's bedroom window.

"Mee Maw?" Billy rapped his knuckles against the window. He could see her bed on the far side of the room, as far from the window as possible.

"Mee Maw?" Billy tapped louder. His thumb ring pinged sharply against the glass. "Open the window."

He sensed movement underneath the blankets. Saw her small white head turn on the pillow. She was only half-awake but staring straight at him. He held up a box of oatmeal pies.

"I brung you Little Debbies, Mee Maw," he said. "A whole dozen!"

His grandmother beamed. "Billy? Is that you?"

"Yes, ma'am, Mee Maw!" His smile looked more like a leer.

"Such a dear, sweet boy."

Mee Maw slowly crawled out of bed, found her slippers, and shuffled to the window.

"*Well done, Billy boy,*" said the voice inside Billy's head. "*Well done.*"

Mary O'Claire sat perched on her bed, nibbling a spongy oatmeal pie.

She smelled the familiar scent.

Brylcreem.

"Who are you?" she muttered to her grandson.

"Me? Why, I'm your grandson. Billy O'Claire." The young man, who didn't sound at all like Billy tonight, sat in an orange vinyl chair next to her bed.

"You're not my grandson!"

"Yes, I am. I'm Billy! Your grown-up grandbaby."

"No. You may *look* like Billy, but that's not who you really are!"

"Is that so?" The evil spirit inside Billy's body made

his wicked grin grow wider. "Well, then, who do *you* think I am?"

Mary trembled. "You're *him*."

"Him *who*?"

Mary put one hand to her chest. She felt her ribs tighten and squeeze most of the air out of her lungs. She knew who was sitting in the room with her.

"You're my husband," she gasped. "Clint Eberhart. I can see his evil in your eyes."

"Well, well, well. You're pretty sharp for a dried-up old biddy," said Billy, speaking the words the dark spirit of Clint Eberhart dictated. "I'm surprised you're still alive. And don't call me your husband. I dumped you a long time ago. Remember?"

"We weren't divorced. . . ."

"Oh? Then why'd you change your name back to O'Claire?"

"After what you did, I couldn't stand being called Mary *Eberhart*!"

"Cut the gas, doll. I don't need to hear your noise."

"You're evil, Clint. Pure evil!"

"Yeah? Well, I could've been evil and rich, but you had to butt in and ruin everything!"

"I told Sheriff Jennings the truth!" Mary whispered. "There were children on that bus, Clint. Children!"

"So? You ask me, you're the one who killed 'em all! If you hadn't called Mr. Spratling, nobody would've died!"

Mary could hear her heart pounding. It sounded like it had moved up to her skull. It sounded like it might explode.

"Sheriff Jennings knew everything, Clint. I finally told him—after he shot my son."

"Son? Wait—let me guess. You married some other sap?"

"I never remarried, Clint. My son was your son."

"That's impossible!"

"The night you died, I was six months pregnant."

"No, you weren't! I never had no son!"

"Yes, you did. You just never met him."

"You're lying!"

"No, Clint. Lying is a sin."

"Really? The nuns teach you that?"

Mary nodded.

"So how come you never told me about this baby?"

"Because you abandoned me, Clint. When you and Mr. Spratling cut your deal!" Mary shook her head. "No wonder my boy went bad. Like father, like son!"

"Shut up, you old hag!"

"No!" It was Billy. The real Billy. Fighting back. He wanted to hear more. Learn about his father. His grandmother could sense that he was struggling to regain control of his body.

She smiled gently. "Are you in there, Billy? If so, remember that I love you. No matter what."

"*Shut up!*" Eberhart was back. "*No more talking!*"

Eberhart's spirit made Billy's body rise from the chair. Made him stretch out his arms and moan so fiercely that it shook the windowpanes and knocked a drinking glass off the bedside table.

"Die, old woman!" he roared. "Die like you should've died fifty years ago on that bus!"

Then Clint Eberhart allowed his real body to materialize inside the room. He became a mushrooming cloud of red-hot rage hovering over Mary O'Claire. He moved his ghostly hands toward the old woman's throat as if he would strangle her.

It was enough to scare Mary O'Claire to death.

That week's front page of the *North Chester Telegraph* ran a feature story about Mary O'Claire.

"MIRACLE MARY" DIES

NORTH CHESTER—"Miracle Mary" O'Claire, the sole survivor of the Greyhound bus accident of June 21, 1958, died in her sleep at the County Rest Home on Monday night.

She was called Miracle Mary because she walked away from the infamous bus wreck that killed 38 passengers, the driver, and the occupant of the Ford Thunderbird it collided with. She was the only survivor.

Miracle Mary boarded the Greyhound Scenicruiser in Massachusetts. When the bus neared North Chester, it was broadsided by a

Ford Thunderbird convertible driven by a Spratling Clockworks employee named Clint Eberhart. Mr. Eberhart had been traveling south on Highway 31. The bus was headed east on Route 13. A state motorcycle trooper was also killed that night, raising the total number of casualties to 41.

The accident, still the worst in county history, led to public safety hearings and the installation of a blinking red light at the crossroads of 13 and 31.

After escaping the bus wreck uninjured, Mary O'Claire disappeared from the public spotlight. Her son, born three months after the accident, later achieved his own notoriety.

In 1983, at the age of 25, Thomas (Tommy) O'Claire and his wife, Alice, were gunned down by Sheriff James Jennings in what was described as the "tragic and fatal conclusion to a bungled blackmail scheme." The shootings took place outside Spratling Manor.

Miracle Mary is survived by one grandson, William O'Claire, a plumber who still works in the North Chester area. Mr. O'Claire could not be reached for comment.

Zack stood barefoot on top of the rock jutting out over the swimming hole.

"Jump in, sport!" Davy floated in the water below. "There ain't nothin' to be scared of!"

"I didn't see *you* jump in!" Zack shouted to Davy.

"Don't worry. Water's over ten feet deep. You won't crack open your head bone!"

"But the water's freezing!"

"Wait for the sun. Here it comes. Clouds are partin'! Jump, Zack! Jump!"

For the first time in his life, Zack did something he knew was extremely foolish. He went running across the slick stone and kept running after he reached its edge.

"Geronimo!" He plunged feetfirst into the frigid pool and sent up a foamy geyser.

It was dark and cold underwater. Zack should have

been terrified, but instead he felt exhilarated. His toes touched the slimy creek bottom, so he pushed off and kicked his way back to the surface.

"Whoo-hoo!" he screamed through a rush of bubbles when he sprang up. "Whoo-hoo!"

"By jingo, you did it, Zack! You dove off Dead Man's Bluff."

"I want to do it again!"

"All rightie. Have at it!"

Zack swam to the shore and hauled himself out of the water. The pockets of his cargo shorts bloated out into water balloons.

"This time, I'm gonna do a cannonball!"

Zack clambered up the cliff and took off running. He leapt and kicked and climbed into the air. He tucked his knees up to his chest and screamed as he plummeted into the briny depths of the bounding main. He smacked the top of the water with a stinging, thumping whack.

"Whoo-hoo!"

When Zack bobbed back up to the surface, he saw Davy in the woods, pulling on his overalls.

"Hey, where you goin'?" In the distance, Zack could hear a bell softly chiming.

"Pops is ringing the bell. Must need me to do some chores."

"What? It's Saturday. Nobody works on Saturdays."

"Farmers do."

"Oh. But what about the big plan?"

"You know what we need next."

"Sure, but . . ."

"You'll find it just where I said."

"But . . ."

"What's wrong, Zack? Somethin's troublin' you, I can tell."

"Promise you won't laugh?" Zack climbed out of the pond and pulled his T-shirt off the branch where he had hung it.

"Cross my heart and hope to die."

"Well, what if . . ." Zack hesitated.

"What if what?"

"What if Kyle Snertz sees me?"

"That don't make no nevermind."

"It doesn't, hunh?"

"That boy's all wax and no wick. If he gives you any guff, just give it right back."

"How?"

"I reckon you could always pants him."

"*Pants* him?"

"Yes, sir. Just pull down his trousers and show everybody his underwear! That usually works."

"Really?" Zack sounded doubtful.

"Or you could give him a wedgie. Tug real hard and pull his underpants up into his butt crack."

"I see."

Zack wished Davy had some better ideas on how to defend himself against Kyle Snertz. Ideas that didn't involve underwear.

"Pants him or pull a wedgie, hunh?"

"Yes, sir. Either one will do the trick."

The bell tolled louder in the distance.

"Jiminy Christmas, I best run. See you later, pardner!"

Davy scampered up the hillside and disappeared into the forest. That meant Zack would have to face his demons alone.

Especially the one named Kyle Snertz.

42

Judy sat on the back porch with the newspaper, a yellow legal pad, and a big jug of sun tea.

George was at his office in New York—even though it was Saturday—making final arrangements for his trip to Kota Kinabalu, Malaysia, on Monday night. Zack was off playing with Davy. Judy was ready to start working her puzzle.

On her pad, she had already jotted down some notes from her conversation with Gerda Spratling: June 21, 1958. Clint.

Now she added some items she had circled in the newspaper story about Miracle Mary O'Claire: Greyhound bus accident. June 21, 1958. Thirty-nine dead on bus. Clint Eberhart dead in Thunderbird. Motorcycle cop killed. Intersection of 13 and 31.

She sipped some tea.

Miss Spratling's Clint had to be this Clint Eberhart. He died after his car collided with the bus in the crossroads.

She remembered something else Miss Spratling had said: "They ran him off the road."

Probably up the embankment and into the oak tree.

She wanted to go find Bud. The neighbor who had helped fix her flat tire. He worked for Greyhound. Maybe he knew more of the story. She also wanted to go see Mrs. Emerson down at the library, see what she could find in the local history books and old newspapers.

Zack and Zipper came running into the backyard. Zipper's paws were muddy, his underbelly a collection of matted muck. Zack's shorts were dripping wet.

Okay. The puzzle may have to wait until after a load of laundry.

"How'd you guys get so soaked?"

"Davy and I found a secret lagoon."

"Really?"

"Actually, I think it's a cow pond."

"I like the sound of 'lagoon' better," said Judy.

"Yeah. Me too."

"Bet it felt good. On a hot day like this."

"Yep. Real good."

"Well, why don't you clean up Zipper, then run inside and put on something dry."

"Okay."

"You want to go down to the library with me later?"

"Maybe. Can I grab something to eat first?"

"Oh. Sure. I can make you a sandwich."

"That's okay. I'll just, you know, fix it myself."

"I promise I won't toast, bake, or broil."

"I'll just do a PB and J. And then I might take a shower."

Judy grinned. "You don't want to go to the library, do you?"

"Not really. Not today. I mean, it's Saturday and all."

"You're right," Judy said. "Go get cleaned up."

"Okay."

Zack ran into the house.

Judy glanced back at her notes.

June 21.

June 21 was the summer solstice. The longest day of the year. The shortest night.

1958.

Fifty years ago this Wednesday.

She wondered if Miss Spratling had anything special planned for the anniversary.

Zack found the dog's towel hanging in the mudroom and swiped it under Zipper's belly before he grabbed the dog by the collar.

"Sorry, Zip. You need to wait upstairs."

Zipper dug his hind legs into the thistle rug and tried to sit down while Zack tried to pull him forward. Finally, Zack scooped Zipper up, cradled him in his arms, and carried the dog upstairs to his bedroom. He didn't waste time changing into dry shorts or taking a shower. He closed the door and stood in the hall.

"I'll be right back," he said through the door. "And remember—no barking!"

Zipper barked.

"Zipper?"

Zack heard whimpering on the other side. But no more barks.

He raced down the steps and went to the front hall to retrieve the hacksaw he had hidden in the closet the night before. Since Judy was still out on the back porch, he slowly opened the front door, careful not to let it make any noise—even when he eased it shut again. Once outside, Zack turned right and ran toward a house being built three doors up the block.

He saw a pile of neatly stacked lumber, but Zack wasn't interested in free wood today. He scaled the cinder-block foundation and trotted across the decking to find the treasure hidden out back.

There it was, just where Davy had said it would be: a shiny steel toolbox tucked up against the foundation.

Zack jumped down to the cement-splattered clay and examined the lock. Davy had told him its shackle was made with a "cut-resistant alloy" and warned Zack that it might take half an hour to hacksaw through it.

But we need the galdern tool!

That's why he added a shower and a sandwich to the list of things he supposedly needed to take care of inside the house. Judy wouldn't start wondering where he was for thirty, maybe forty-five minutes.

Zack started sawing. A thin dust of metal filings hit the dirt near his knees. Five minutes later, his hair was soaking wet from exertion, but the cut was only an eighth of an inch deep. He might be out here for over an hour.

Judy will come into the house looking for you! Saw faster, pal! Faster! Give her some galdern elbow grease!

Zack took in a deep breath and, grunting, put everything he had into his hacksaw thrusts. A drop of bubbly sweat fell on his knee.

It took Zack an instant to realize it wasn't sweat.

It was spit.

"What you doin' down there, Barbie?"

Zack looked up.

Kyle Snertz loomed over him. The sneering bully hawked up another slimy wad, juiced his lips, and let loose a thick chunk of spit. The spew smeared across Zack's glasses.

"I said, what are you doin', *Bar-bie*?"

"Nothing" was the best Zack could come up with.

"Hah!"

Snertz leapt down. His three buddies came bounding down after him.

"Well, well, well. Barbie here is trying to bust into a toolbox."

"No, I'm not."

"That's *my* toolbox. We got first dibs."

One of Snertz's cronies held a heavy-duty bolt cutter with three-foot-long handles.

"I only need one tool," said Zack. "You guys can have the rest. Okay?"

"Hah!" said Snertz. "All the tools in that box belong to me! I need 'em to build a railroad."

Zack was confused. "A railroad?"

"Yeah. On your chest!" Snertz shoved Zack backward, knocked him to the ground, sat on his stomach, and started pummeling his rib cage.

"First we need to crush the rocks!"

"Hey! Get off of me!"

Snertz pinned Zack's arms underneath his knees.

"I said get off of me, snothead!"

"What? What'd you call me?"

Furious, Snertz ripped open Zack's T-shirt and rasped a knuckled fist up his sternum—leaving behind a raw ribbon of skin burn.

"Get off of me!"

"Uh-oh! Rocks. Little bitty boulders." Snertz twisted Zack's nipples. "We may need dynamite!" He slammed his fists like wet, meaty sledgehammers against Zack's chest and made explosion noises.

Zack refused to cry. The punches and pinches hurt, but he would not cry.

Pants him!

Zack heard Davy's voice in his head, remembered his friend's stupid advice.

"Time to drive in the stakes!"

Snertz found a jagged chunk of concrete broken off the corner of a cinder block. He studied Zack's exposed chest, considered where to scrape first.

"Get off of me!"

With a back-arching thrust, Zack freed his arms,

grabbed Snertz's belt loops, and yanked his shorts down to his knees.

The other boys started to laugh. Snertz's face went fish-belly white.

The bully was wearing diapers! Disposable training pants. Zack saw cute little jungle critters dotting crinkled plastic. Apparently, Kyle wasn't properly potty trained and his parents made him take the necessary precautions.

"Gross, Snertz," one of the boys said. "You wear diapers?"

"Shuddup!"

The other boys started waving the air in front of their faces and laughed even louder.

"No wonder he stinks all the time."

"Hey, pantsload!"

Now Kyle Snertz was the one with a new nickname.

He didn't waste time buttoning his shorts; he held the front flaps together with one hand so they wouldn't fall down while he ran home—probably to hide in his room and cry.

Buh-bye, pantsload!

The other boys stuck around. When Zack told them what he and Davy were planning to do, they were eager to help. They used the bolt cutter to snap open the lock, and Zack pulled out the treasure he had come here to retrieve: a cordless drill with an extremely long, one-inch auger bit.

Zack would bring the drill back when the job was done. But he and Davy really needed the tool for a day or two because it had the kind of bit that could easily bore its way down into a stump.

"Where have you been? You and me need to talk!"

Billy O'Claire sat in his tattered La-Z-Boy recliner. It was midnight and he had been trying to watch TV when Clint Eberhart materialized like some alien beamed up on *Star Trek*.

"What do you mean, where have I been?" asked Clint. "I've been inside your body ever since we went to visit the old lady."

"That was Monday, man."

"So?"

"This is Saturday! Buy a watch, dude. One with a calendar!"

Clint grinned. "You have a bad attitude, boy."

"Yeah. Like father, like son."

Clint moved closer. There was a hungry look in his hypnotic eyes. "I need you, Billy. Need your body."

"So do I. Go get your own."

"Sorry. I'd have to dig it up, and I don't even know where I'm buried."

"Maybe you weren't. Maybe your car was burned to a crisp after it hit that bus and there was nothing left of you but a greasy stain!"

"Doesn't matter. I'll use yours."

"My car?"

"Your body!"

"Sorry. You can't have it. Like I said: I'm already using it."

Clint Eberhart grinned devilishly. "You're flesh of my flesh, blood of my blood, Billy. That's why it's so easy for me to slip inside your head and take control, make you do whatever I want you to do. We're family!"

Now it was Billy's turn to laugh. "Family? You scared my grandmother to death!"

"She should've died decades ago!"

"I take it you two had 'issues'?"

"Mary O'Claire ruined my big score! Why couldn't she just die like everybody else on that bus?"

"Don't know. But, personally, I'm kind of glad she didn't. Otherwise I wouldn't be here right now, would I? And we wouldn't be having this conversation, which I can't believe we're doing, anyhow! I mean, what are you? Some kind of Halloween ghost? A zombie? One of those soul suckers from the comic books? Are you even here now, or am I just going crazy?"

Eberhart narrowed his icy blue eyes. "Tell me about my son."

"Who's he?"

"Your father, lamebrain."

"Oh. Right. What do you want to know?"

"How about his name?"

"Thomas. But most people called him Tommy."

"And your mother?"

"Alice. She and my father both got themselves killed when I was a baby."

"How? How did they die?"

"Cop shot 'em."

"What?"

"On his twenty-fifth birthday, Mee Maw finally told my father who *his* father was. In other words, I guess she told him all about *you* and, for whatever reason, Tommy figured Mr. Spratling owed our family some money, so he set off to collect the cash."

"Go on."

"Tommy and Alice went over to Spratling Manor and demanded to see old man Spratling. The security guards told them to vacate the premises. My father threatened the guards. The guards called the cops."

"And then?"

"The sheriff told Tommy and Alice to go home. Promised he wouldn't press charges. They pretended to walk away."

"And?"

"Well, when they figured the sheriff wasn't looking, they twirled back around and whipped out their weapons!"

"Hot diggity dog! What were they packing?"

"Shotguns. Tommy fired first; then Alice pumped off a round."

"And that sheriff got peppered full of lead, right?"

"No. They missed."

"What?"

"They missed!"

"Both of them? With shotguns?"

"Yeah. I think my parents needed glasses. I know I do sometimes. Like when I watch TV or read the funny pages."

"Billy?"

"What?"

"Tell me what happened!"

"Oh. The sheriff shot back. Tommy and Alice both died. End of story."

"Okay. Okay. Tell me about the fuzz, this sheriff—what's his name?"

"Um . . ."

"Where is he? How do we find him? Because it's payback time, Billy!"

"I think his name began with a J."

"So this is why my spirit never passed over to the other side. Too much unfinished family business to take care of!"

"Sheriff 'Juh'-something."

"We need a plan, Billy! This sheriff—is he still alive? Does he have any family? A son? Maybe a grandson? Billy? What are you doing?"

"Thinking."

"Well, hurry up!"

"Okay. Yeah. I remember. His name was Jennings. Sheriff James Jennings."

"You ready for another?" George Jennings stood over the griddle, flipping Sunday-morning pancakes.

"Okay, just one more," Judy said after taking a big gulp of milk.

"Zack? How about you?"

"Sure!"

Zack's dad flipped two fresh pancakes onto his plate.

"You know," he said, "it's a law that all American fathers must make pancakes for their families one morning every weekend."

Judy giggled between bites. "Really?"

"Oh, yeah. It's in the Constitution. The Founding Children put it there."

Zack rolled his eyes. "The Founding Children?"

His dad moved back to the bowl to give the batter another good whisking. "Yep. They were sort of like the

Founding Fathers, only, you know, younger. I believe it was twelve-year-old Benjamin Bartholomew Bisquick who penned the pancake proclamation." He tapped the box of pancake powder. "Family business and all that."

Judy was laughing too hard to chew. Zack shook his head and smiled.

And people thought *he* had an overactive imagination.

After breakfast, Zack, his dad, and Zipper went out into the yard to check out the progress on the tree house.

"Wow. Neat."

Zack's dad looked up at the crooked collection of lumber and plywood nailed helter-skelter to the limbs of a tree.

"Is that the door?" He pointed at a triangular space where three sheets of plywood didn't quite meet.

"That's a porthole."

"Unh-hunh. I see. Neat."

A blue plastic tarp was hanging over the top of the structure.

"That the roof?"

"Now it is."

"Unh-hunh."

"Sometimes it's our sail."

"Zipper go up there with you guys?"

"Yep. We built him an elevator." Zack pointed to a plastic mop bucket tied to a yellow nylon rope.

"Well, you boys certainly have been . . . busy."

"Yeah. Davy's good with construction projects. He thinks up the plans. I do most of the work."

"Unh-hunh . . ."

"We like the way it looks. Sort of like a ship. Judy went into town and got us the pirate flag."

"Cool. So where'd you guys get all the wood and stuff? Judy drive you out to Home Depot?"

"Nope. Scrap piles."

"Scrap piles?"

"From the construction sites. It was free because it's scrap."

"Zack? That's a brand-new sheet of plywood."

"We were told we could take anything we wanted."

"And exactly who told you that?"

"The aluminum-siding man."

"Who?"

"The tin man."

"Are you making this up?"

"No. We met an aluminum-siding salesman in the forest across the highway and he said—"

"A tin man? In the forest? Is this *The Wizard of Oz* all of a sudden?"

"No. It's true. A tin man is what they call aluminum-siding salesmen."

"Zack, no one has sold or used aluminum siding since 1959!"

"Well, Mr. Billings still sells it. Clarence W. Billings, and he said—"

"Zack? Stop. Enough."

"Yes, sir."

"I'm very disappointed in you, Zachary. You cannot steal wood from construction sites. However, you *can* go to jail for petty larceny. You can also cost me my law license if the court finds me to be an accessory to your felonious behavior."

"But we didn't *steal* the wood."

"Yes, you did, and, frankly, you only make matters worse when you lie and say you didn't."

"But, Dad—"

"This is what you do, isn't it? Make up complicated stories to cover your tracks. Tin men. A traveling salesman named Clarence W. Billings—"

"But, I—"

"Your mother told me about this. 'He's making me sick with his silly, childish jokes and stories.' "

"Judy said that?"

"No. Your real mother. Susan." He took a deep breath. "She was in pain and there was nothing I could do. I'd try to cheer her up, but cancer is very serious business, son, and—"

And then his father choked on whatever words he wanted to say next.

Zack could see him straining to hold back tears.

"Okay, Zack," his father finally said. "Here's what we are going to do. You and I are going to make a list of every piece of 'scrap' you stole and where you stole it.

Then we are going to drive out to Home Depot and purchase replacements. The cost will be deducted from your allowance until the balance is paid in full. Is that clear?"

"Yes, sir."

It was absolutely, completely, 100 percent clear: His mother's ghost had definitely followed them up to Connecticut.

46

Judy drove over to the North Chester Library when Zack and his father took off for Home Depot.

"What brings you here on such a gorgeous Sunday?" Mrs. Emerson asked. "Researching your next book?"

"No. Remember how you told me that you didn't know why Miss Spratling put her memorial on that tree behind our house?"

"Yes, dear. I remember. In fact, I have a very keen memory. My knees are shot, but my memory is just fine. Now, then—what have you discovered about Gerda Spratling's shrine?"

"What do you know about the Greyhound bus accident of June 21, 1958?"

"I know how to find out more. After all, dear, I am a librarian."

= = =

An hour later, the two women sat at a large table covered with clothbound volumes of old newspapers.

" 'The Greyhound Scenicruiser was on its usual route from Boston to New York,' " Mrs. Emerson read from the lead news story in the *North Chester Telegraph.* " 'Along the way, it picked up campers from Camp Stillwaters. . . .' "

"A Boy Scout camp?" Judy asked.

"No, dear. A Bible camp. Used to be dozens up this way." She tapped at a list printed alongside the main story. "This is the passenger manifest. Mostly strangers who had never met and they end up spending eternity together."

"You think they're linked in the afterlife because they died together?"

"I do."

"Why?"

"Read, dear. We'll discuss my ontological speculations later."

"Ontological?"

"The metaphysical study of the nature of being and existence."

"Oh. Right."

"Read, dear. Read."

Judy studied the list.

GREYHOUND SCENICRUISER
BOSTON–NEW YORK
AND ALL LOCAL STOPS
PASSENGER FATALITIES
June 21, 1958

1. Pfc. Sylvester Barrows, 19 years old,
   U.S. Army
2. Clarence W. Billings, 36 years old, salesman
3. Sister Mary Ignatius Brady, 45 years old
4. Millicent Chapman, 9 years old, camper
5. Elizabeth Erin, 10 years old, camper
6. Dorothy Fenwick, 10 years old, camper
7. George Fenwick, 8 years old, camper
8. Christopher Ferguson III, 29 years old
9. George S. Gladding, 37 years old,
   businessman
10. Rebecca Goodwin, 18 years old,
    high school student
11. Corp. Simon Gorham, 22 years old,
    U.S. Army
12. Pfc. Alfred Grabowski, 20 years old,
    U.S. Army
13. Calley Jordan, 9 years old, camper
14. Mr. James F. Karpen, 43 years old,
    insurance salesman
15. Mrs. Charlene Karpen, 37 years old
16. Jessie Karpen, 10 years old

17. Harry Karpen, 8 years old

18. Gideon Leet, Jr., 10 years old, camper

19. Hudson Leverett, 9 years old, camper

20. Susan Lund, 10 years old, camper

21. Dr. William Mitchell, 35 years old,
    college professor

22. Mrs. Maryann Mitchell, 32 years old

23. Cody Mitchell, 5 years old

24. Hailey Mitchell, 5 years old

25. Tamara Mitchell, 6 months old

26. Pfc. Amos Morgan, 18 years old, U.S. Army

27. Sister Beatrice Mulligan, 55 years old

28. N. C. Perry, 76 years old, retired

29. George Porter, 8 years old, camper

30. Catherine Pratt, 8 years old, camper

31. William E. Selden, 9 years old, camper

32. Reverend Edgar Stiles, 48 years old

33. Sister Elizabeth Synnott, 63 years old

34. Charles Wannamaker, 38 years old, scientist

35. Russell White, 46 years old, businessman

36. Kathleen Williams, 31 years old,
    nightclub singer

37. Daniel J. Wilson, 28 years old,
    auto mechanic

38. Sgt. Abraham Yates, 29 years old, U.S. Army

39. Pfc. Adam Zahn, 19 years old, U.S. Army

40. DRIVER: Bud Heckman, 35 years old

Judy stared at the list to make sure she saw what she thought she saw.

Bud Heckman, the driver, was a local, so the newspaper ran his photo in the column alongside the list. Judy recognized him immediately: the nice man who had told her how to change a flat tire. Her goose bumps sprouted goose bumps. No wonder she had met the helpful man so close to a graveyard.

Bud Heckman was dead.

Zack and his father didn't speak during the twenty-minute drive to Home Depot. They didn't speak while they pushed the rumbling orange cart around the cavernous warehouse or when they loaded it up with plywood sheets, two-by-fours, two-by-twelves, and one twenty-foot-square blue vinyl tarp.

Finally, when the lumber was tied down to the luggage rack on top of their car, Zack broke the silence.

"I'm sorry, Dad."

"I'm sorry, too. We should have come out here last weekend."

"I guess."

"Well, tomorrow I'm staying home from work."

"Really?" Zack tried to sound excited.

"I think they owe me the day, don't you? I mean, I have to leave at night and spend all day Tuesday on an airplane."

"Yeah."

"I could help you guys hammer in a few nails."

"I hope you're not mad at Davy. None of this was his fault."

"I don't blame Davy. He seems like a good kid."

"He's awesome. We were even thinking about having a campout."

"Really? Up in your pirate ship?"

"Yeah." Zack hung his head. "But I guess I'm kind of grounded. . . ."

"Well, I think you've learned your lesson. So do you guys need supplies for this campout?"

"Really? Do you think we could buy a kerosene lantern?"

"Wouldn't propane be better?"

"Kerosene is more like what a pirate would have. With the wick and all. More old-fashionedy."

"I see. Okay. Let's go back inside and see if they have a lantern."

"How about one of those fuel cans?"

"Good idea." His father smiled. "You know, I had a kerosene lantern when I was your age."

"Really?"

"Yep. And you're right. It does look more like what a pirate would have."

An hour later, they returned home with the building supplies, a lantern, and a red plastic canister filled with two and a half gallons of kerosene.

Now Zack and Davy had everything they needed.

Judy decided to just ask.

"So tell me, Mrs. Emerson, do you believe in ghosts?"

The librarian didn't miss a beat. "Of course I do, dear. Then again, I have a slight advantage over you. I've actually seen a few. Six to be precise."

"Ghosts?"

"Yes, dear. We were discussing ghosts, weren't we?"

"Yes, but—"

"Oh, they're nothing to be afraid of. Just one more piece of information to process. A new realm to explore."

"You're saying you've actually seen a ghost?"

"No, dear. I said I actually saw six. It was forty years ago. Late May. Early June. Mr. Emerson and I weren't married. Just dating. I was nineteen. He was twenty-one, had a car. One Saturday night, he took me for a drive down this back country road so we could watch the submarine races."

"The what?"

"We went there to neck, dear. To make out? We parked near a cornfield not far from the crossroads. We saw nothing but moonlight and fireflies until the Rowdy Army Men appeared."

The Rowdy Army Men. Grandpa's favorite ghost story.

"Six drunken soldiers stumbled out of the forest like a small herd of deer. They weaved their way into the darkened field, waved their weapons, and swigged hooch from brown paper sacks. One soldier eventually spied us watching and, as quickly as they came, the six men disappeared. They vanished into a foggy mist."

"I've heard about these army men," Judy said.

"Yes. They're quite the local legend. Children dress up as Rowdy Army Men on Halloween. Well, not the little children. The teenagers. The ones who find it funny that six drunken soldiers home on leave shot each other and died in a Connecticut cornfield instead of on a Korean battlefield."

"Is that how the story goes?"

"Yes, dear. Although I don't believe it to be true."

"You don't?"

"Of course not. However, I do believe the six men did, indeed, die together, which is why they must spend eternity together."

"Scaring teenagers in lovers' lane?"

"It's not really a lane. More like a dirt road. Since

that night, I have made quite a study of paranormal phe-
nomena. At first I assumed that the field was a portal. A
door for spirits to pass through as they journey from
their world into ours."

"Okay."

"Then I wondered: Was it a residual haunting? That's
the most common kind."

"Really?"

"Oh, yes. The residual theory suggests that a building or a piece of earth holds the psychic impression a
person made when they were alive."

"I see."

"But then again, this could be a traditional haunting.
The soldiers didn't pass over at the time of their death
because some sort of unfinished business held them
back."

"Wait a minute," Judy said.

"Yes?"

"You said that these six soldiers shot each other?"

"No. I didn't say that. That's simply what the local
legend would have us believe."

"Okay. But in order for that legend to be true, two of
those army men had to fire *and* get shot at the same
instant. The last two men had to kill each other."

Mrs. Emerson smiled. "Exactly. I like the way you
think because it's precisely what I thought! It's also why
I never went along with the conventional wisdom. Those
soldiers didn't shoot each other."

"No?"

"No, dear. You see, I am old enough to remember this Greyhound bus accident in the crossroads." Mrs. Emerson tapped the newspaper. The passenger manifest. "Take a closer look, dear. The answer is right there. Read the list of names."

Judy did.

Mrs. Emerson smiled. "Pay particular attention to passengers one, eleven, twelve, twenty-six, thirty-eight, and thirty-nine."

Judy read the names: " 'Private First Class Sylvester Barrows, Corporal Simon Gorham, Private First Class Alfred Grabowski, Private First Class Amos Morgan, Sergeant Abraham Yates, Private First Class Adam Zahn.' They're all U.S. Army soldiers."

Mrs. Emerson nodded. "Six soldiers. Six ghosts. The Rowdy Army Men were all passengers on the same bus. They died together; they now spend eternity together."

"Well, then," said Judy, "I guess your ghosts know my ghost. Mr. Bud Heckman. He was their driver!"

Billy O'Claire sat in his trailer, staring at the blade of a butter knife.

Someone had carved a message into the stainless steel.

Unfinishd biznis.

Billy knew he had probably scratched the words into the knife himself. Probably used a paper clip. Maybe a chunk of gravel from out in the yard.

But if his hands were responsible for etching the words, he wasn't the one choosing them. It was the other guy, his newly discovered grandfather.

It was early Monday morning. Billy's head throbbed and his teeth felt slimy. He hadn't showered or shaved for a couple of days. He was a stinky, stubbly-faced wreck. But he was alone.

Alone!

Clint Eberhart, the evil spirit, wasn't with him! Wasn't inside him!

Billy had to think.

Who else does Eberhart want dead?

He already gave Mee Maw a heart attack. Now he wants to hunt down this Jennings family. But what about the rest of the O'Claire clan? What about me?

And Aidan!

Oh, no. What about Aidan? What if he wants to kill my son?

Billy raced over to Spratling Manor.

He saw his ex-wife's car parked out front in the same circular driveway where his parents—Tommy and Alice—had been shot twenty-five years earlier.

Billy hated this place, but he had to do this, had to do what was right. He had to protect his son.

An antique Cadillac crawled out from behind a vine-covered brick wall. Billy climbed down from his pickup truck and hurried across the weedy driveway to confront the chauffeur.

"Excuse me? Sir?"

The sleepy-eyed old man tilted his head slightly.

"I'm looking for Sharon."

"What?"

"Does Sharon still work here?"

"Who?" The chauffeur looked confused.

"Sharon!" he shouted at the old man.

"Billy?"

Sharon was on the front porch. She was dressed in a puke green nurse's smock.

Billy ran over to her, but she gave him the palm of her hand.

"Hold on, Billy."

He froze.

"How many times do I have to tell you? I don't ever want to see you again!"

"I know. But you've got to listen to me. Just this one last time."

"Billy," Sharon said impatiently, "it's Monday and we need to take Miss Spratling into town and then out to her memorial. If you have something to say, you better say it fast!"

"Don't ever let me near my son." He said it as quickly as he could. "Don'teverletmenearmyson!" He repeated it even faster.

"I don't get this, Billy. Ever since the divorce, you've been pestering me: 'Let me see Aidan.' Now you're telling me to keep you away?"

"Yes! No matter what I say. No matter what I do. Don't let me anywhere near Aidan, okay?"

"My, my, my. Who is this?"

The old bag, Gerda Spratling, appeared on the porch behind Sharon. She was wearing some sort of long black gown and a black veil that covered her face. She raised it to smile flirtatiously at Billy and give him a queasy stomach.

He tried hard to smile back. It wasn't easy to do when a wrinkled old prune was giving you goo-goo eyes.

"Sharon?" Miss Spratling crowed dryly. "Who is this handsome young man? Your boyfriend, perchance?"

"No, ma'am." Sharon's ears burned red. "I don't have a boyfriend."

"Well, that doesn't surprise me. Not in the least. You are rather homely." Miss Spratling took a step forward. "Have we met before?" she asked Billy. "You look so familiar . . . especially around the eyes."

Billy took off his sweat-stained baseball cap. "I'm just a friend of Sharon's."

"A friend, eh?" The old lady hunched her head toward her shoulder. "My, my, my."

"Well, I have to go."

"So soon?" Miss Spratling fluttered her eyelids. "You will call again, won't you, Mr. . . . I'm sorry; I don't believe I caught your name."

"O'Claire. Billy O'Claire."

Gerda Spratling cringed at the name.

O'Claire. Just like Mary O'Claire—the lying gutter-snipe who walked off that bus and told all those horrible lies about Clint Eberhart.

She should have hated anyone named O'Claire.

But this charming boy named Billy was just too hand-some to hate—almost too handsome to resist.

With such soulful blue, blue eyes.

Judy decided not to tell anybody else about the ghosts.

It would only scare Zack, and her new husband didn't really believe in "goofy stuff" like goblins and ghouls. Even if George didn't think she was crazy, Judy still didn't want to talk to him about ghosts because he had one of his own. So did Zack. In fact, they shared the same one. How could you talk to people about the ghosts you thought you'd chatted with when they both wished they could talk one more time with just one: their late wife, their dead mother?

The ghost sightings would remain Judy's secret. If she needed to talk to somebody about it, Mrs. Emerson would be more than happy to oblige.

Judy was out in the woods near the big stump, tamping down the soil around a newly planted rosebush, when George came out to join her.

"Hey," she said. "All packed?"

"Yeah. What are you up to?"

"Putting in a couple rosebushes."

"Neat. Have you seen Zack? I promised him I'd pound a few nails before I took off for the airport."

"He and Davy went swimming again. They have a secret lagoon."

George smiled. "Really? I had one of those when I was his age."

"I think this one's really a cow pond."

"Yeah. Mine was, too. There was this big boulder you could dive off of. We called it Dead Man's Bluff."

They heard the crunch of gravel under tires—cars pulling off the road.

"Well, here she comes," Judy said. "Right on schedule."

George peered through the trees, down to the highway. "I remember seeing that Cadillac when I was a kid. They used to drive it up the middle of the road. Thought they owned the streets as well as everybody's souls."

"George? Behave. Promise?"

"Yes, dear."

There were three cars parked on the shoulder of the highway this week. The Cadillac, the Hyundai, and a new addition, a maroon Lincoln Town Car. Judy saw the feeble old chauffeur climb out of the big-bumpered Caddy and shuffle around to the right rear door.

A dark-haired young priest stepped around to the

trunk of the Lincoln and disappeared under the lid. When he emerged, he was carrying a four-foot-tall resin statue.

"Oh, boy," mumbled George. "Is that a birdbath?"

Judy shushed him.

"Hello again," Judy called out cheerfully as Miss Spratling and the priest trudged up the woodsy slope to the stump. "Beautiful day, isn't it?"

"Mrs. Jennings," the old woman said. Her voice was dry ice.

"What a pretty statue," Judy said to the priest, a man she had never met before.

"Thank you," he panted.

Miss Spratling cleared her throat. Loudly.

"Oh, I'm sorry," said Judy. "Miss Spratling, I'd like you to meet my husband, George Jennings. He grew up here in North Chester."

George extended his hand. "I'm very pleased to finally make your acquaintance, Miss Spratling."

Miss Spratling clucked her tongue. "My, my, my. You're just like your father, aren't you? All la-di-da and polite. Just like your father."

"Excuse me?"

The old woman pointed her gnarled finger at Judy's new planting. "What is that?"

"A white rosebush."

"Pull it out of the ground this instant! That's where the statue is meant to go!"

"Whoa!" said George. "Take it easy, Miss Spratling. My wife was simply trying to—"

"I will not have you two defiling sacred ground!"

"And I will not have *you* telling us what we can and cannot do on our own property."

"This is not your property, Mr. Jennings! Clint Eberhart purchased this soil with his soul!"

"Is that so? I'm a lawyer, so I'll need to see the deed and title report."

Miss Spratling scowled, then seethed.

The priest dabbed his brow with a linen handkerchief. "I just came to bless the statue," he said. "To commemorate the fiftieth anniversary."

"The anniversary of what?" George demanded.

Miss Spratling's lips quivered.

"The accident," said Judy.

"It was no accident, you foolish little girl! I remember what that bus driver did to Clint." She glared at George. "I remember what *others* did to my father!"

"Look, it's okay, George," said Judy. "She can put her statue there for the celebration."

"Celebration? Why, you ignorant, ill-bred child!"

"Hey!" George shot back. Judy cut him off with a shake of her head.

Miss Spratling knotted her fists. "There is nothing here to celebrate!"

"I'm sorry, I meant—"

"You wait. You'll see. One day, your husband here

will drop dead and you will be forced to go on living—knowing that you will never, *ever* see him again. When that happens, will you *celebrate,* Mrs. Jennings? Will you decorate your home with gaily colored balloons?"

"Okay." Judy had heard enough. "We're going inside now. You can pull up the rosebush. You can tear out everything. You can do whatever you want."

"My, my, my. Aren't you congenial?"

Then Miss Spratling grabbed the thorny rosebush with her black-gloved hands and ripped its roots right out of the ground.

51

Zack and Davy saw and heard everything.

They had come back from the swimming hole and were hiding in a thicket where they had a leaf-framed view of the Wicked Witch and her priest.

"So, pardner," Davy whispered, "you think that statue is made out of plastic?"

Zack watched as the priest twisted the statue down into the loose dirt.

"Sure looks like plastic." Zack heard a hollow *plunk* when the priest banged its pedestal against a rock. "Sounds like plastic, too."

"Swell. That means the galdern thing will melt. It'll melt real good."

The old lady crawled back inside her Cadillac and was driven away. The other cars drove away, too.

"Okay," said Davy, "we'll be ready in a couple days."

"Is that enough time? There's so much to do."

"Just bore them holes like I shown you. Soak her good with the kerosene. She'll be ready to go."

"You'll help, right, Davy?"

In the distance, the boys once again heard the farm bell tolling.

"Aw, shucks. It's Pops. Jiminy Christmas, seems he rings that dang bell every time we're all set for an adventure!"

"Don't go, Davy."

"Have to, Zack. Pops would tan my hide if I don't come when he rings the bell."

"I can't do this without you."

"Sure you can. In fact, you can do it better than anyone. That's why I chose you."

"No. Wait. If you knew who I was . . ."

"You're Zack Jennings."

"No . . . I mean who I really am . . . what people say about me . . . what my mother . . . I screw things up, Davy. I ruin everything for everybody!"

"Zack?" said Davy. "I don't rightly care what folks say about you. What they say can't make you who you are—'less, of course, you let 'em."

The bell clanged louder in the distance. "Wait! Don't go, Davy. Okay? Stay."

"Can't, I reckon. But don't worry. I'll be back. I promise."

Zack needed more. "Cross your heart?"

"Yep! And hope to die!"

52

About an hour later, George fixed Judy a tuna fish sandwich.

"Why does she have to be so mean?" she asked.

"I think it runs in the family. Besides, some of the locals say the Spratling money is almost gone. I guess she's bitter about that and her dead boyfriend—even though that was fifty years ago and you'd think, you know, she might have worked that one out by now."

"I don't want her coming out here every Monday, ripping up our flowers."

A bassy thumping came thundering from the backyard. An angry man grunted and rhymed.

"What's that noise?"

"Either the end of the world," said George, "or rap music."

Judy was at the window. "It's Zack."

"No way. Zack likes rap?"

They saw Zack and Zipper at the edge of the trees. Zack smiled and waved. Zipper wagged his tail. There were three other boys, all about Zack's age, hanging out around a boom box.

"Who are all those other kids?" Judy asked.

George recognized the boys from the empty lot. "Neighborhood kids. Looks like our shy guy has made some more new friends."

"Pump up the volume," Zack said to the boy manning the boom box.

The four boys hiked down the trail toward the stump.

"The music will cover any noise the drill makes. I'll do the first hole. Then we'll take turns."

Zack pulled the cordless drill with the forty-inch auger bit out of his nylon gym bag. The boys would drill to the depth that Davy had specified. Later they would fill the holes with kerosene.

They'd pour in at least two and a half gallons—more if they could scrounge it up from their camp lanterns and their parents' space heaters. With time, the kerosene would soak down into the wood and seep into the deep roots. If all went according to plan, the stump would be burned out of the ground before next Monday.

Before the old lady came back to hurt Judy's feelings again.

A *little* before four p.m. that same day, Billy O'Claire drove his pickup truck into the Rocky Hill Farms subdivision. He needed money so he could get away from his grandfather's ghost, maybe head down to Florida. He stroked his hand through his sweaty hair and remembered the house with the gurgling toilet. He had never really finished that job. He should go back, talk to the owner, tell him he needed to do more work on his sewer lines, the main one in the basement, if he seriously wanted to stop the problem from reoccurring.

The owner would cut him a deposit check, might even give him cash. Of course, Billy would never come back to finish the job. He wouldn't be able to: He'd be in Florida, hiding from Grandpa's ghost.

=   =   =

"Car! Zack yelled when he heard somebody pulling into the driveway. "Tarp!"

Two of the boys draped a big blue sheet over the stump to hide the holes. The boy currently manning the drill stuffed it back into the gym bag, then tossed the sack to another boy waiting up in the tree house, who stashed it behind a sliding panel of plywood.

The boys had all seen a lot of prison escape movies and knew how this sort of thing was supposed to be done.

"Howdy, son," Billy said politely, holding his grungy baseball cap in his hands. "Is your mom or dad home?"

Zack stood with his hands on his hips. Zipper was at his side, ready to pounce.

"Dad?" Zack hollered. "Dad?"

His father came out to the back porch. "What's up, Zack?"

"This guy's here. The plumber."

"Hey, great! I've been meaning to call you. I think we should take a look at the main drain—which I think is also our main pain."

Billy nodded. "Yes, sir. That's why I swung by. I was thinking the same thing. We might need to snake out the pipe leading to the street."

"Exactly! Can you come back and do the job?"

"Yes, sir. Early next week."

"Great."

"Of course, I'll need to rent a bunch of special equipment."

"I could give you a deposit. Say fifty percent now, fifty percent when the job is done. Would that help?"

Billy smiled. "Yes, sir. That would help a whole bunch."

Billy sat in the kitchen, sipping a cold Coke the man had given him while he ran off to find his checkbook.

Florida, here I come!

He felt a little bad about ripping this guy off, taking money for a job he knew he'd never finish. Heck, he wouldn't even start it. He'd be on his way to Miami before the sun went down, which made him happy and sad at the same time. Happy that he was protecting his son. Sad that he'd probably never see his boy again.

All of sudden, he thought he could smell some of that minty gunk his ghostly grandpappy slicked through his hair. Then he saw a bowl of foil-wrapped candies sitting on the kitchen counter. Peppermint patties. Man, he had to get out of North Chester. Fast. The whole town was messing with his mind.

He stood up, eager to hit the highway. He was going to call out to the guy hunting down the checkbook until he realized he didn't even know the man's name. The general contractor who'd built the house had paid Billy for all his previous work. The job was always called "14

Stonebriar." Never the "Jones House" or the "Smith House."

Not knowing what to say, Billy went with the generic.

"Uh, excuse me? Sir? Sir?"

The man came into the kitchen. "Sorry," he said. "Took me a minute to find the checkbook."

"No problem, sir."

"Please, call me George."

"Okay, George. I'm Billy. Billy O'Claire." Billy stretched out his arm to shake George's hand.

"George Jennings."

Billy blinked.

"Jennings?"

"Yeah."

"We used to have us a sheriff up this way named Jennings. Sheriff James Jennings?"

"I know. He was my dad."

"Really?"

"Yep."

"Your daddy was Sheriff Jennings?"

"Yep. He sure was."

Billy grinned. "Well, I'll be. Ain't that something? Ain't that just like crazy, daddy-o?"

Clint Eberhart's soul had zoomed back inside Billy's body and he was now using it to shake hands with George Jennings—the son of the man who had killed his son!

"Are you okay?" asked Zack's father.

"Fine and dandy, just like cotton candy." Billy's smile was suddenly very wide.

"Here you go." Mr. Jennings handed Billy a check. "You sure you're okay?"

"Oh, yeah. Never better."

George waited for Billy to leave. Billy stood there rocking up and down on his heels.

"Shouldn't you go cash that check? Rent the equipment?"

"Right. Good idea."

The spirit of Clint Eberhart made Billy's body go sit in the cab of his pickup truck and wait. Another minute. Maybe two.

When Eberhart was certain that Mr. Jennings had gone back to whatever he had been doing upstairs in the house, his angry soul forced Billy's legs to walk down the driveway toward the woods, down to where he could hear the boys playing.

Slip down the side of the house, Billy. We're gonna go kill the Jennings boy. Yes, indeedy. My grandson's going to kill the sheriff's grandson.

Billy's feet resisted. Eberhart exerted more force.

Come on. Get a move on! Shake your bunny tail, boy!

Billy plodded into the backyard with his mouth drooping open in a dull circle. He reached the path leading into the patch of trees.

"Can I help you, mister?"

A boy with an aluminum baseball bat blocked Billy's path.

"Who are you?" Billy asked. "Mickey Mantle?"

"Who's Mickey Mantle?"

"Slugger for the Yankees? Led the major leagues in home runs, RBIs, *and* batting average back in '56?"

The boy looked at Billy as if he was nuts.

"Tarp!" he yelled over his shoulder.

"Tarp!" several voices echoed from the woods.

"You're not allowed back here."

"Why not?"

"Mr. O'Claire?"

Eberhart swiveled Billy's head back toward the house and saw Mr. Jennings.

"I thought you were leaving."

"I'm trying to," Clint had Billy say. "But I got turned around. Which way's the driveway?"

Jennings pointed left.

"Thank you." Clint made Billy whistle while he walked up to his truck. He knew he'd be coming back here soon.

Real soon.

He'd be back to take care of some unfinished family business.

He'd be back to kill the Jennings boy.

55

On Monday night, Zack's father flew off to Malaysia.

Judy was secretly glad George would be out of town and out of reach for almost a week. It would give her more time to learn all she could about the other passengers on the Greyhound bus. Maybe one night she'd even go check out the graveyard, see if Bud was still there, see if any of the Rowdy Army Men were with him.

George might be on his way to an exotic foreign country, but Judy knew she was venturing someplace far more exciting!

Early Tuesday, Zack and his new friends were in the backyard playing. Judy brought the boys a snack.

"Where's Davy?" she asked Zack.

"Farm chores."

"Aren't you glad we don't live on a farm?"

"Yep."

"I'm going to the library. I'm taking my cell phone if you need me."

"Okay."

"Stay in our yard while I'm gone, okay?"

"Okay."

"My mom's home," one of the other boys said. "She'll keep an eye on us, too."

"Great. Okay. Am I forgetting anything?"

"Nope. I don't think so."

"Great. Have fun!"

Judy kissed Zack on his forehead. Zack stepped back, wiped the wet spot off his brow. The other guys sort of looked away, scuffed at the dirt with their shoes.

"Oops," Judy whispered to Zack. "Not cool?"

"It's okay."

"I won't let it happen again."

"Have fun at the library, Judy."

"I will."

Judy made a mental note: *Only kiss stepson when no other boys are present.*

"Thank goodness you're here!" the librarian said. "Come into my office."

Judy followed Mrs. Emerson into a small room.

"Look what I found!" She pointed to several cardboard boxes stacked on her desk. "Well, it's really two things. Which do you want first?"

"How about the first thing?"

"Excellent choice. Thing number one: old police logs." She pried open a box. "When the North Chester Police moved to their new building, they sent us scads of archival information. Boxes and boxes of it. Most of it is junk. Old gun magazines and equipment catalogs and . . ."

"And?"

Mrs. Emerson pulled a dusty ledger from the box.

"The call log for June 21, 1958. A minute-to-minute accounting of the day's events. See? The North Chester Police received a report of a suspicious person harassing the Greyhound bus at 9:20 p.m."

"Who made the report?" Judy asked.

"The call came from the driver, Mr. Bud Heckman. Apparently, he had a two-way radio. He also informed the police that a woman passenger was in danger, so he was . . ." Mrs. Emerson ran her finger under a line in the ledger. " 'Fleeing the scene at a high rate of speed.' "

"And so?"

"The North Chester Police contacted the state police, who dispatched an officer on motorcycle. Let me see . . . yes . . . Officer Mike Mulgrew. You'll find his name cited in several newspaper reports about the accident. He died at the scene with all the others."

"So," Judy asked, "what was the second thing?"

"Ah, yes. While performing my research, I noticed something rather peculiar: We are not the first to investigate this incident."

"Oh?"

"I kept noticing the same name on prior requests for the same information."

"Who?"

"Your late father-in-law, Sheriff James Jennings. Twenty-five years ago, he was looking at everything you're looking at today."

Late Tuesday afternoon, Zack and the boys finished drilling.

There were so many one-inch tunnels sinking down into the stump, it looked like a giant wheel of Swiss cheese. Zack put the drill back into the toolbox at the construction site before Davy even touched it.

"Summer's the busiest season on a farm," Davy explained when he showed up after the other guys had gone home. "So many chores, it's a wonder I'm still alive!"

"Whatever," Zack said. He placed a big rock on the edge of the tarp covering the stump.

"Hey, pardner—you ain't mad at me, are you?"

"Well, maybe. A little. You come up with all these big plans, but you're never around to do any of the work!"

"I know. I know. Like I said, Pops has been—"

"And what about the kerosene? What if it explodes? What if there's spontaneous combustion or something? We need someone who's done this kind of thing before, someone who's worked with kerosene and stumps and . . ."

"Like a farmer boy who's cleared him a field or two in his day, hunh?"

"That's right. We need you, Davy."

"Zack, you're right. We'll do her tonight!"

"What?"

"You and me, pardner. We'll soak in the kerosene tonight!"

"Really?"

"Yep! Here's how we'll swing her. We'll tell your stepmom we're camping out up in the tree fort. She'll go for that, right?"

"I guess."

"Sure she will. Shucks, she'll probably even cook us a late-night snack!"

"No way."

"How come?"

"Judy doesn't cook. She's from New York City."

"Here you go, boys." Judy put two Burger King sacks into the mop bucket. "Whoppers, fries, and chocolate shakes. And some Milk-Bones for Zipper. You can let him have some of your burgers, but no onions, okay? It'll make him gassy."

"Thanks!" Zack hoisted the snack up to the tree house. Zipper pranced on his hind legs. Zack unwrapped a burger and placed it on the floor, back where Judy couldn't see Zipper having a feast, onions and all.

"Of course, Zipper's sleeping with you guys tonight," Judy said, "so what do I care if he, you know, gets *gassy*? *Real* gassy."

Zack realized "gassy" was a grown-up word for "fart." He tried to pull the Whopper away, but Zipper's front paws had already trapped the wrapper.

"Do you have your lantern, Zack?"

"Yep."

Judy saw the big gas cans sitting on the ground under the tree house.

"Do you need that much kerosene for one lantern?"

"We might," Zack said. "Especially at night. In the dark and all."

"You never rightly know," Davy added. "Best to be prepared."

"Okay. But don't stay up *too* late, promise?"

"Promise," said Zack.

"Have fun, boys."

"We will, Mrs. J.!"

Judy noticed the shadowy tarp draped over the stump. It was propped up to a pup-tent peak by the plastic statue's head.

"What's with the tarp?"

"Well, Mrs. J., I heard what that galdern old lady said to you."

"You did?"

"Hard not to, what with her hollerin' and all. I heard every nasty word that old witch had to say."

"Now, Davy . . ."

"Ma'am, if you ask me, folks shouldn't ought to say things like that. Dwellin' on the sad parts of life when you ought to be livin' each day and bein' happy. So, if you don't mind, we'd rather not have to look at her galdern stump and statue all week long."

Judy smiled. "Good night, guys."

"Oh, Mrs. J.? Can Zack sleep over at my place tomorrow night? I asked Pops and he says it's okay by him if it's okay by you."

"Well, we'll see. Let me check with Zack's father when he calls tomorrow. Good night, boys."

When Zack was certain Judy was gone, he turned to Davy.

"I get to sleep over at your place tomorrow? Neat!"

"Well, that's the little white lie we'll be telling your stepmom. Meanwhile, I'll tell Pops I'm sleeping over here."

"Is this another part of the plan?"

"Yep. Just because I ain't been doin' any drillin', don't mean I ain't been doin' any thinkin'."

"Cool! Want a burger?"

"No, thanks. I ate at home."

Zack munched a few salty fries. Zipper padded over, hoping for seconds.

"You sure you don't want a burger?"

"Positive. Let Zipper have at it."

"He'll fart."

"I reckon he might. Just don't light a match nowheres near his butt if he does."

"Yeah, he might make the kerosene explode!"

"Dang right! And we don't want that to happen—not till tomorrow."

"Tomorrow?"

"Yep. Why do you think we're planning us that sleepover date?"

Judy had hired a babysitter, Nicole Murray, a teenager recommended by Mrs. Emerson.

"Keep an eye on the boys, but try not to let them see you. I don't want them to think I think they're babies who need a sitter."

"I'll stay inside unless I hear something."

"Great. And help yourself to anything in the fridge."

"Okay. What if I need to reach you?"

Judy handed Nicole a slip of paper. "Call my cell."

"Cool. So where you going?"

"The graveyard."

"Really? At night?"

"Yeah."

"Awesome."

=   =   =

It was ten p.m. when Judy pulled out of the Rocky Hill Farms subdivision and merged onto Highway 31.

When she reached the crossroads, she turned left.

She headed west for a couple hundred yards, then eased onto the soft shoulder in front of the graveyard, stopping in the same spot where she and Bud had fixed that flat tire

Judy knew from reading the old newspapers that this was the Haddam Hill Cemetery and that Bud Heckman was buried here. None of the others who died that night were laid to rest in North Chester, but their spirits roamed around near the crossroads because that was where they had died. It didn't really matter that some, like the Rowdy Army Men, were buried as far away as Indiana or Tennessee. Their ghosts still haunted Connecticut.

Judy switched on her emergency flashers. She didn't have a flat tire but thought if she pretended to be in automotive distress, Bud might show up again like he had that first time.

Judy's eyes quickly adapted to the darkness. She looked up the hill. Weeds and tall grass grew between weathered headstones. A spiked fence penned in the rectangular plot. Angels with frozen stone wings topped a few monuments.

A car came up the road. Its headlights made Judy squint. When the lights passed, she could see that it was a truck, not a car. Some kind of pickup. It didn't stop. Judy was relieved.

She looked up at the graveyard.

Still nothing. No Bud. No army soldiers stumbling around the headstones. No bony skeleton hands poking up through crumbling topsoil like they always did in the movies.

Judy stepped out of her car and onto the gritty shoulder of the highway. The night was warm, the moon full. Crickets screeched their noisy lullaby. She walked into the field, felt long strands of straw whip against her jeans.

She looked up the hill and saw the shadowy outline of a tall man.

Behind the fence.

He moved quickly and carried some sort of satchel: a small suitcase like you might take with you on a Greyhound bus trip from Boston to New York!

The man slipped out of view when he crossed behind a shed-shaped mausoleum.

Judy moved faster, crouched lower. She made her way to the fence and heard voices. Giggling. The man and now a woman. Not in the graveyard. Beyond it. Near the fence on the far side. Judy crept past the corner post and saw two silhouettes sitting on the ground, pointing up at the stars.

"Hello?" Judy called out. "Is anybody there?"

A woman's voice answered: "Judy?"

Oh, no—one of the ghosts knows my name!

"Is that you, dear?"

A battery-powered lantern snapped on. Judy saw Mrs. Emerson sitting with a thin man in his sixties. They were eating sandwiches wrapped in wax paper.

"Mrs. Emerson?"

"Hello, dear. Care for a deviled egg?"

"No, thanks. . . ."

It was a picnic basket, not a suitcase.

"We came out," Mrs. Emerson said, "to see if there were any souls doomed for a certain term to walk the night."

"That's *Hamlet,* right?" the man said.

"Actually, dear, it's the ghost of Hamlet's father."

"I mean, it's from *Hamlet.*"

"Yes, dear. Judy, allow me to introduce my husband, Henry Emerson."

"Most folks call me Hank."

"That doesn't make it right, dear."

"How long have you two been out here?" Judy asked.

"Since sundown," Mrs. Emerson said.

Mr. Emerson winked. "She told me we were coming out to watch the submarine races."

Judy smiled. "Seen anything interesting?"

The Emersons stood, brushed specks and flecks and burrs off their pants.

"Nothing," Mrs. Emerson said.

"Too bad. Maybe tomorrow?"

"Indeed. After all, tomorrow will be the fiftieth

anniversary of the bus accident. But tonight? Not a soul is stirring."

Mr. Emerson winked again. "You might say it's totally dead!"

Judy went home, paid the babysitter, checked on the boys and the dog asleep in the tree house, and then went upstairs to bed.

She had forgotten all about the pickup truck that had passed by the graveyard earlier. It was now parked very close to the crossroads.

Waiting.

58

Zipper started barking.

Zack woke up. Looked at his watch. It was three a.m.

"What is it, Zip?"

Zipper barked again. Zack struck a match and lit his lamp.

"Lose the lantern," Davy ordered. "Somebody's coming. Somebody bad."

Zack twisted the knob to extinguish the flame.

"Put Zipper in the bucket." Davy remained remarkably calm. "Lower him down."

"All by himself?"

"We're heading down, too. Don't worry, pardner. Everything's gonna be okay." Davy said it with cocksure confidence. "You first. Down the ladder. I've got you covered." Davy pulled out his slingshot. "Hurry, pal. He's coming."

Zack swung his feet around and found the ladder. He skipped a few boards on the way down and landed hard.

Davy was already on the ground and held a finger up to his lips. "Shhh."

The boys could hear the *ping ping* of aluminum bouncing against aluminum. Davy used his right hand to gesture "to the left and down."

The clanging came closer. So did the voice of a crazy man who sounded a lot like the scary street people Zack remembered from New York City, the ones who marched up and down the sidewalks screaming at themselves.

"Up the hill! *No!* Do it. *I can't!* Chicken! *Shut up!*"

Davy slipped silently under the trees without so much as snapping a twig.

Zipper started barking again.

Zack turned and, in a bright shaft of moonlight, saw the plumber guy who had been at the house earlier—only now he was dragging a ladder, its pulley rattling against the rungs. *Ping ping. Ping ping.*

The plumber stopped, saw the boys.

Zack saw the insane look in the guy's eyes.

The knife dangling off his belt.

"This way!" Davy rambled down the slope toward the highway. Zack and Zipper ran after him.

Billy dropped the ladder and chased after the boys. He slipped on a wet patch of leaves, lost his legs, landed on his butt.

"Get up!" the spirit of Clint Eberhart insisted.

"No!"

"Come on, Billy boy—get up off the ground."

"No! You can't make me do this!"

"Kill the Jennings boy and we're done. I promise!"

"Up there!" Davy cried as they ran up the highway.

"Where?" Zack was winded. If they had to run much farther, he knew he'd be lying in the middle of Route 13, wiggling and kicking like an upside-down bug.

Davy ran faster.

"Head for the graveyard, pardner!"

"What? Are you crazy?"

"Nope. But that feller chasin' us sure is!"

Zack dared a glance over his shoulder. The plumber was less than a hundred yards away. Zack saw a knife blade flash in the moonlight. He ran faster.

"He's afraid of graveyards!" Davy said when they reached the iron fence.

"Why?"

"Most bad eggs are."

"Really?"

"You bet."

"How come?"

"What'd'ya say we hop over the fence first and discuss it later?"

"Yeah. Sure."

"Climb on over. Zipper can squeeze through the bars."

Zack wished he were better in gym class, better at running or scaling walls or climbing ropes. There was no way he could pull himself over the fence.

"Let's go around to the gate. . . ."

"Ain't got time."

"I can't do it."

"Sure you can."

"I'm no good at—"

"Hush. Use the crossbeams like a ladder!"

Davy pointed and Zack saw how he might be able to scramble over the wall.

"There you go. Easy does it. One foot at a time and alley-oop!"

Zack hauled himself up and over.

"Way to go!" Davy was waiting for him on the other side. Zipper had made it, too. "You should of seen ol' Zip slipping through them bars!"

The plumber was still coming, still screaming.

"Follow me," Davy said. He led Zack through the gravestones and into the deep shadow of a mammoth tomb topped with a concrete cross.

"We'll be safe back here."

"How come?"

"Sacred ground."

"Hunh?"

"The crazy ones are always scared of sacred ground."

Zack looked around. They were near the gate. It was wide open.

"The gate! It's open!"

"Don't worry, pardner. He can't come in."

Zack couldn't see the maniac plumber anymore, couldn't hear his screams or his threats. All he could do was hope that Davy was right about sacred ground and that the plumber knew the rules, too.

Billy stopped running when he reached the cemetery fence.

"I want to go home," he groaned. "Now."

"Shut up, you big baby!" he yelled at himself in the voice of Clint Eberhart.

"I need to go home," said Billy. "I'm exhausted."

"You're like a broken record! I swear I ought to—"

"There will be no swearing, young man. This is sacred ground."

Three nuns were standing behind the fence—three penguins in flowing black robes with winged white wimples on their heads.

"Nuns?" fumed Eberhart. *"I hate nuns!"*

"Hate can be very dangerous, Mr. Eberhart," said the shortest nun. "Hate will doom you to hell for all eternity!"

"Hah! I ain't never going to hell, Sister. I'm going to live forever!"

"No man lives forever."

"Oh, yeah? Just watch me, doll!"

The oldest nun spoke even more serenely than the first.

"Mr. O'Claire? Mr. William O'Claire? Can you hear me? I know the demon spirit has taken control of your body, but I hope you are in there, too. Mr. O'Claire, my name is Sister Elizabeth Synnott."

"Sin-snot? What kind of name is that? Do people call you Sister Boogers?"

"Billy?" said Sister Elizabeth. "Listen carefully. Your grandmother forgives you for what the evil spirit forced you to do."

"What?" Billy heard the nun through the fog that always came whenever Eberhart took charge of his body.

"Mee Maw forgives you, Billy. She told me that you were a good boy. That you visited her in the nursing home and brought her oatmeal pies and—"

"Shut your mouth!" Clint snarled through Billy's lips.

But Billy fought back.

"Sister, tell Mee Maw I—"

"Hate her guts for turning me into such a pansy!" Clint's spirit was stronger.

"Go home, Billy," Sister Elizabeth said gently. "Resist the demon. Can you do that for your Mee Maw?"

"I'll try, Sister."

"One last thing, Mr. O'Claire."

"Yes, ma'am?"

"Watch over your son."

Eberhart yanked Billy's head sideways, wrenched his neck out of joint, sent spasms wriggling through his limbs.

"You have a son, Billy boy?"

Sister Elizabeth gasped. Understanding dawned. "I'm sorry, Billy," she said. "I didn't realize—"

"Why is this the first I'm hearing about my great-grandson?"

"Keep him away from Aidan!" the nun implored.

"Why, Sister, what a horrible thing to say! Keep me away from my great-grandson? This Aidan and I are family."

60

Early Wednesday, Judy sat in the breakfast nook with a cup of coffee and not much else.

She needed to hit the grocery store. Soon. She saw the checkbook sitting next to the empty fruit bowl. It was too early to go outside and wake the boys. Besides, she had nothing to serve them for breakfast. Maybe she could run out to the store and grab some doughnuts, cereal, and fruit. They'd be okay for fifteen minutes.

She opened the checkbook to rip out what she assumed would be check 001.

It was 003. George must've written two checks. She looked at the stub flaps. Check 001 went to Mandica and Son for the tree work. Check 002 was made out to Billy O'Claire. The plumber.

So that's his name. O'Claire. Just like—

Judy put down the checkbook, went to the small

kitchen office, and found the clasp envelope where she kept all the notes and clippings she'd been collecting. She pulled out the Miracle Mary newspaper story and raced down to the last paragraph:

Miracle Mary is survived by one grandson, William O'Claire, a plumber who still works in the North Chester area.

He still works here, all right—right here in this house. Judy remembered something else from that story. Some kind of connection between O'Claire and her husband's family. She skimmed up a few paragraphs to the part about Mary's son.

In 1983, at the age of 25, Thomas (Tommy) O'Claire and his wife, Alice, were gunned down by Sheriff James Jennings in what was described as the "tragic and fatal conclusion to a bungled blackmail scheme." The shootings took place outside Spratling Manor.

Zack's grandpa had killed the plumber's father and mother. Did the plumber know that George was the sheriff's son? He certainly now knew that George was a Jennings. He had to. It was written in the upper left-hand corner of the check.

Was the plumber's working at their house merely coincidence or part of some clever scheme for revenge?

Judy felt a sudden pang.

Maternal instinct? Do stepmothers get that, too?

She didn't know where it came from. All she knew was she had to go check on Zack and Davy in the back-yard and she had to do it now!

Zack wasn't in the tree house. Neither was Davy or Zipper.

Judy saw a paint-splattered aluminum ladder lying in a small clearing. On its side was stenciled O'Claire's Plumbing.

She was right! She might also be too late.

Sheriff Hargrove was at the house three minutes after Judy dialed 911.

"They were sleeping in the tree house," Judy told him. "They're in trouble. The plumber, Billy O'Claire. He's Miracle Mary's grandson." She pointed at the ladder.

"But why would—"

"George's father killed Tommy and Alice O'Claire."

"The plumber's parents?"

"Exactly."

"What's that smell?" Hargrove sniffed the peppery air.

"Kerosene." Judy saw Zack's lantern shattered on the ground. "They must have dropped it." Judy scanned the backyard, saw some bent branches. Footprints. "They ran that way. The dog went after them." She pointed at paw prints in the mud and then a grooved indentation left by a big boot. "So did the plumber." Judy saw more dog tracks. "This way," she said.

"Wait a second. It might be best if—"

"This way!"

The sheriff followed Judy down a trail the boys had ripped through the underbrush. When they reached the highway, they saw the plumber's pickup parked on the shoulder.

"Stay back. Behind that tree there. Now. Go."

He approached the vehicle. "Mr. O'Claire? Mr. O'Claire?"

There was no response.

"He's not here!"

Judy squinted, looked up and down Route 13.

"See that tall grass near the graveyard?" she said. "It's been trampled down!"

"Yeah." Hargrove started jogging. Judy ran after him. She was faster.

"Zack?" Judy yelled between breaths. "Zack!"

A dog barked.

"Zipper?" she called out.

The dog barked louder. Judy and the sheriff crested cemetery hill. She saw Zack standing behind the railings.

"Zack!"

Hargrove ran around the fence, found the gate. Judy worked her arms through the bars so she could hug Zack.

"Are you okay?"

"Yeah. Fine."

"Where's Davy? Is Davy okay?"

"Davy went home," Zack said. "The farm bell rang. He had chores to do."

Sheriff Hargrove worked his way through the graveyard and stood next to Zack and Zipper. "Are you okay, son?"

"Yeah. It was the plumber. He wanted to kill us, so we ran away."

The sheriff scanned the horizon. "Where'd he go?"

"I don't know. We hid behind a tombstone all night long."

"Good for you!" said Judy.

She silently vowed that she'd never let Zack out of her sight again, not until he was eighteen—no, twenty-one!

Judy and Zack sat in the breakfast nook, eating peanut butter and jelly sandwiches. Zack had a tall glass of cold milk, Judy iced tea. Zipper lay patiently on the floor, dreaming about peanut butter stuck to the roof of his mouth.

"Your dad should be calling soon," Judy said.

"I'm sorry I ran away."

"You did the right thing."

"Dad will just think I'm a scaredy-cat."

"No, he won't."

"Do we have to tell him?"

"Well, I think he'll want to know."

"He thought I wouldn't go into her room because I was scared to see her dying and all."

"Your mom?"

"Yeah. She hated me."

"No, she didn't, honey. She had cancer and they were giving her all sorts of medicines and that can make people say and do—"

"Judy?"

"Yes?"

"My mother hated me before she ever got sick." Zack fiddled with the crust on his sandwich.

"You want to tell me about it?" Judy asked.

"You won't think I'm just making it up?"

"No."

"Promise?"

"Cross my heart."

"Okay. I never told anybody any of this. Not even my dad."

"You can tell me."

Zack realized maybe he could. "Okay. My mom said I made her life miserable and stole my dad away from her. And the cigarettes that killed her? She only smoked them on account of me. Cigarettes were the only pleasure she had left in her whole life, and the more miserable I made her, the more cigarettes she had to smoke. So I tried to stay away from her, honest, I did, especially when she got the cancer, so she wouldn't have to smoke so much but she said even when I wasn't there she could still see me because she had minions—these evil servants who spied on me. Like the Wicked Witch has those flying monkeys, my mom had her minions so she could always see what I was up to."

"Did your dad know about any of this?"

"No. She told him I was a big baby who made up silly stories. She said I told fibs because 'all liars are cowards,' afraid of the truth. She'd tell him she was trying her best to be a good mother, but I just made it impossible."

"What about your grandpa?"

"He never visited us in the city much. We mostly came up here, and Mom usually wasn't feeling good whenever we did, so me and Dad came up without her."

"Nobody knew?"

"You're the second person I ever told."

"Who was the first?"

"Davy."

Judy smiled. "He's a good friend, isn't he?"

"Best I ever had."

"Well, Zack, your mother is gone. She can't hurt you anymore. I promise."

"But she probably sees us right now even though she's dead. She probably hears me saying mean things about her. And when I laugh and stuff? I know it makes her mad. When I hang out with Davy and Zipper and we go to our secret swimming hole and the sun feels so good, my mom gets even madder. She hates me having all the fun I stole from her. You know, I wouldn't be surprised if she's the one who sent that plumber after us, like maybe she invaded his body and used him like a robot to come get us because she can't do it herself anymore."

The telephone rang.

Judy rubbed her moistening eyes with the back of her hand and picked up the phone.

"Hello? Hey! How's Malaysia?"

Zack stared at Judy. He looked terrified.

"Us? We're fine. Zack and Davy camped out in the tree house last night. Oh, they had a blast. Tonight he might spend the night over at Davy's house. Say, have I ever thanked you for giving me such a great son? Well, thanks again. You want to say hi? Hang on, honey."

Judy passed the phone to Zack. She nodded to let him know everything was going to be okay.

"Hey, Dad. Nothin' much. Hanging out with Davy and Zipper and Judy. . . ."

He didn't mention the kerosene-soaked stump.

Or the box of Ohio Blue Tip matches he had hidden in his gym bag.

Two police officers delivered a moldy cardboard box to the Jennings residence that night around eight p.m.

Judy was sitting on the front porch, sipping a glass of wine. Zack was upstairs in his room, playing video games. Zipper was with him.

"What's this?" Judy asked.

"The chief found this box buried in the back of a closet in the old building. Didn't send it to the library with the other stuff because it appears to be personal items from when Mr. Jennings was sheriff. Sheriff Hargrove figured you folks might like to have it."

Judy smiled. "Probably Grandpa's old socks."

"Probably."

"So have you guys apprehended Mr. O'Claire yet?"

"No, ma'am. We would've brought this box over earlier, but we've been dealing with that situation."

"I understand."

"Well, we better roll."

"Be safe."

"Thank you, ma'am."

The two cops trooped down the steps and into their cruiser. Judy examined the box. The top was sealed with gummy duct tape. Water stains spread up from the cardboard bottom. She opened the flaps and was hit with the unmistakable scent of mildewing newsprint.

More clippings.

The box was crammed full of newspaper stories about the 1983 incident at Spratling Manor.

Judy did some quick math in her head. She figured the plumber was probably in his mid-twenties, so he must've been born right before Grandpa shot his parents. The boy had basically been orphaned when he was an infant and had probably been plotting his revenge all his life.

She read a yellowed headline: *Bungled Blackmail Scheme at Spratling Manor.* She skimmed the article. Apparently, Mary O'Claire's son, Tommy, tried to extort money from Julius Spratling. Security guards called the police and Sheriff Jennings responded to the scene.

The perpetrators discharged their weapons, the article reported. *The sheriff returned fire and killed both intruders.*

Judy had that feeling again.

She called 911.

The operator patched her through to Sheriff Hargrove's cell phone.

"I have a hunch about where O'Claire's headed next."

"Where?"

"Well, first he came after Zack, the only descendant of James Jennings currently in town."

"Who do you think is next on his list?"

"The only living descendant of the man who called the police."

"Gerda Spratling?"

"Exactly."

"I'll look into it. Thanks!"

Hargrove clicked off. Judy went back to the papers in the box.

More of the same.

Details about the extortion scheme but no indication of what the O'Claires had used to blackmail Mr. Spratling. Judy pulled the papers out of the box and stacked them on a side table. She looked back into the cardboard carton to make certain she had everything.

Sitting on the bottom, wedged in the seam between flaps, was a small key, the kind that usually opens a bank safe-deposit box.

She pried it out and made another phone call.

"Mrs. Emerson? Judy Jennings. I hope this isn't a bad time." Judy rotated the small key so she could read the inscription on its crown. "Do you know anyone at North Chester First Federal?"

She did.

Mr. Emerson, her husband, was the bank's head of security.

64

Billy O'Claire hid in the woods all day and into the night.

After chasing the boys into the graveyard, he fought hard against the evil spirit that had invaded his body, just like the nun had said Mee Maw wanted him to. Eberhart eventually left and Billy crept deeper into the forest and followed a creek downhill until it met up with the Pattakonck River. He shadowed the river for a mile or two and ended up behind Spratling Manor at the family's ramshackle boathouse. Billy opened its creaky doors, slipped inside, and, exhausted, fell asleep.

The sun set around eight-thirty.

That was when the soul of Clint Eberhart returned.

"Hello, Billy boy. It's time for me to meet your son."

Clint made Billy stumble up a crumbling garden path and rip a fistful of wildflowers from a tangle of weeds.

They headed for the single illuminated window in Spratling Manor.

"This window is absolutely filthy," Miss Spratling said to Sharon. "Remind me to fire your mother!" She paused. "My, my, my. Hello. Isn't that your boyfriend?"

Sharon whirled around.

Billy was leering through the window over the kitchen sink.

"Well, well, well. Invite him in, dearie. Invite him in."

"No!"

"Oh, don't be such a wet blanket!"

Billy held up the clump of wildflowers.

"My, my, my. It appears that young Prince Charming has brought you flowers!" Miss Spratling gestured grandly to her right. Billy slipped away from the window.

"Miss Spratling, I don't think we should let him—"

"Don't be such a big baby, Sharon. Honestly."

A tense moment later, Billy sauntered into the kitchen. "Hey, Gerdy. What's shakin'?"

Miss Spratling's heart fluttered. Only one man had ever called her Gerdy: Clint Eberhart!

"Hey there, Shari baby."

No one had ever called Sharon Jones Shari. Not Billy. Not anyone.

"Who are you?" Sharon stepped back.

"Who am I?" The man laughed. "Why, I just happen

to be the proud father of your bouncing baby boy." He put on his cutest, dimpled smile. "We were married for a while. Remember, dolly?"

Embarrassed, Sharon nodded. "Yes."

"You two were married?" Miss Spratling fanned herself. "My, my, my, Sharon. Keeping secrets? My, my, my."

"I need to see my boy, Shari. Need to see Aidan real bad."

"No."

The man pursed his lips. "Purdy, purdy please?"

"No."

Sharon remembered Billy's plea: *"No matter what I say. No matter what I do. Don't let me anywhere near Aidan."*

"Why do you wish to see Aidan at this hour?" Miss Spratling twirled a strand of stringy hair around her wrinkled finger. "What's your tale, nightingale?"

The man smiled a devilish grin. "Do you know where my boy is, Gerdy?"

"Miss Spratling, please," begged Sharon. "Don't tell him!"

"Of course I know where Aidan is, dearie. I know everything."

"Good. 'Cause I need to see my boy. Need to see him real bad."

"Get out of here, Billy! I mean it! Leave!"

Billy laughed. "I need your son, Shari. This Billy

body is no good for me anymore. Won't do what I tell it to do."

He lunged at Sharon.

She kicked over a chair and ran.

Sharon dashed through the pantry, darted right, and raced across the dining room.

She veered left and headed down a long hall into the old ballroom. There were doors on all sides of the vast, empty space. She took the one that would take her past the library, through the portrait gallery, into the foyer, and out to the driveway. Once outside, she'd race to the carriage house and save her son.

Sharon realized she had only one advantage over her pursuer: She knew her way around the ratty old mansion in the dark; he didn't. But she could hear Billy behind her. Stumbling. Cursing every time he crashed into furniture.

Sharon made it to the front door. As she grabbed the doorknob, she felt a push.

Someone was on the other side, trying to get in!

Had Billy crawled through a window? Was he outside?

Sharon let go of the knob and backed away from the door.

"Hello?" came a man's voice from the other side. "Is somebody there?"

"Yes?" Sharon was shaking.

"I'm Sheriff Ben Hargrove with the North Chester Police," said the voice. "May we come in?"

"Yes. Please! Hurry!"

"Ma'am, we have reason to suspect that—"

"He's here!" Sharon screamed. She could see there were three police cars in the driveway.

"Billy O'Claire?"

"Yes! He's here!"

Hargrove turned to a female officer standing behind him in the doorway. "Mary Beth?"

"Got her. Ma'am?" The female officer grabbed Sharon and escorted her out of the building.

Hargrove pressed a button on his walkie-talkie.

"Jimmy?"

"Yes, sir?"

"You and Dave cover the side. Keep an eye on the windows."

"Will do."

"Springer?"

"Yes, sir?"

"You and Bull cover me. I'm going in."

"Ten four."

"The woman is secure," the female officer's voice crackled from the walkie-talkie. "I'll cover the front door."

Hargrove pulled out a high-intensity torchlight and moved forward. He stepped into a dusty corridor that looked like it might be the Spratling family gallery. Ancient portraits lined all the walls.

"*You like the paintings?*" Eberhart made Billy O'Claire snarl.

Hargrove swung his light to the right.

O'Claire was standing in front of a painting. He held a knife.

"Drop the weapon. We have you surrounded."

Billy jammed his blade into a crusty canvas portrait of Julius Spratling and tugged down to slice a long gash through the dignified old man's head and chest.

"*Cheapskate! Old man Spratling was a penny-pinching welsher, never paid people what they were owed!*"

"Mr. O'Claire, put down the knife." Hargrove raised his weapon.

Billy's eyes twitched. "Shoot me! Please? Stop me!"

"Drop the knife and nobody needs to shoot anybody."

"You don't understand. It's the only way." He gagged. "*Don't listen to this coward!* I can't take this anymore! *Shut up!* Shoot me!"

Billy dropped the knife and clutched his head. "Shut up, shut up, shut up!"

Hargrove holstered his pistol and reached behind his back for a pair of handcuffs.

"*What do you think you're doing, fuzz?*"

"Let's take this nice and easy."

"*No way, copper! You'll never take me alive!*"

"Freeze!"

Billy ran to the foyer, where he saw the swirling red lights of police cars pouring in through the open front door.

"Freeze!" he heard Hargrove yell.

Billy didn't freeze. He raced out the front door. He was going to end this once and for all. He was going to save his son!

The police took him down with a single bullet. Billy O'Claire died in the driveway of Spratling Manor—right where his father and mother had died twenty-five years before him.

The phone rang. Judy snatched it up.

"Hello?"

"Mrs. Jennings? Ben Hargrove. I just wanted to let you know we got him."

"Mr. O'Claire?"

"Yes, ma'am."

"You have him in custody?"

"No. He's dead. You were right. He came after Miss Spratling. He sounded crazy. Talking to himself. And he had a knife."

"I'm sorry you had to—"

"Yes, ma'am. Me too. Anyhow, I thought you and Zack would like to know."

"Thank you."

= = =

Judy knew there was still one piece of the puzzle missing. She also knew she held the key to cracking it.

Literally.

She squeezed the tiny bank key in her hand.

A bright beacon of light swung across the kitchen windows. Judy went to the back door.

"Davy? Is that you?"

"Howdy, Mrs. J.! You remember my pops?"

"Well, I certainly remember his flashlight." Judy shaded her eyes. "Are you okay, Davy? After last night?"

"Oh, I'm fine. How's Zack?"

"Fine." She wondered whether Zack and Davy had had any visitors during their overnight stay in the graveyard. Had Bud shown up?

"We was gonna have us that sleepover at my place tonight," Davy said. "Remember?"

"I'm all set!" Zack stood behind Judy, carrying a small gym bag.

Judy turned to Davy's father. She knew that Billy O'Claire was no longer a threat. If the boys spent the night at Davy's house, she and Mrs. Emerson could check out that safe-deposit box at the bank.

"Sir, are you sure you're okay with the boys sleeping over at your house tonight?"

"Yep," said Davy's father.

Judy knelt down to look Zack in the eye.

"Honey, the sheriff caught the plumber," she said.

"You figured it out, didn't you?" Zack whispered. "You told the police how to catch him."

"Well, I had a hunch. Turns out I was right."

"Thank you!" He hugged her.

Judy thought about how much Zack had been hurt in his short life. There was so much she wanted to say. How she was sorry his mother had been so mean. How things were going to be different now.

But "Have fun, honey" was all she said.

From the look on Zack's face, it might have been enough.

"We will," he said. "Hey, you could use a little fun, too. Maybe you should go see a movie or something. I mean, Dad's not home. I'll be over at Davy's. You and your librarian friend could go out to dinner or the movies or . . ."

Judy smiled. "Don't worry. I know how to have fun."

"You're not going to stay home and watch TV, are you?"

"No. I'll probably go hang out with Mrs. Emerson."

"Zack?" Davy called. "Come on, pardner! We need to find us some good green switches for marshmallow roastin'!"

"I gotta go, Judy. See you tomorrow."

Judy went inside and placed a call.

"Mrs. Emerson? Judy Magruder Jennings. I'm free this evening and I was wondering—do you think you and your husband could meet me at the bank in, say, ten minutes?"

# 67

Zack and Davy waited in the woods until they heard the garage door grind up, then grind down.

"She's off to the movies or Mrs. Emerson's house," Zack said, tugging down on his Mets cap, ready for action.

"Good thing you suggested it, pardner."

"Yeah. But what about your father? Won't he wonder where we are?"

The boys had hung back near the stump while Davy's dad hiked across the highway. The old man had never looked back to see if the boys were following him.

"Pops? Shoot, he's plum tuckered out. I'll betcha he marched straight home, plopped into bed, and forgot all about us. You grab some matches?"

"Yeah." Zack zipped open his gym bag. "I brought the whole box."

Sharon went down to the carriage house and kissed her baby.

"Is this your night off, girl?" her mother asked.

"No. But I had to see Aidan and make sure he was safe."

"He's fine. Look, Sharon—it's a shame about the police shooting Billy, but you need to get back to the big house. Don't give Miss Spratling any excuse to fire us!"

Miss Spratling was waiting in the darkened foyer when Sharon returned.

"Did your mother offer her sympathies on the loss of your ex-husband?"

"Yes, ma'am."

"How considerate. Of course, they all mourn at first.

But then life goes on, doesn't it? After the cards and flowers and condolence calls, they all forget and you're the only one left to mourn his death!"

"Yes, ma'am."

"Come along," Miss Spratling commanded. "We must prepare the chapel. Father Murphy is on his way."

Sharon had never been allowed to enter the Spratling family chapel before. It was also the one room her mother had never cleaned. In fact, no one was ever permitted inside the chapel except Miss Spratling herself. But tonight was the fiftieth anniversary.

Tonight was special.

Judy and Mrs. Emerson were sitting in a conference room, staring at the long metal tray they had removed from the safe-deposit room.

Hank Emerson, head of security for North Chester First Federal, had the second key needed to open the double-locked box. Now he was in the security office, making sure the bank's surveillance cameras were sweeping the parking lot, vault, and lobby while ignoring the conference room.

Judy raised the hinged lid. A brown envelope was tucked inside the narrow box. She undid the flap clasp and discovered what looked like a high school term paper: a typewritten report tucked inside a clear plastic binder with a slip-on spine. The lettering was blurry: a carbon copy off an old typewriter.

Judy knew they had found the missing link.

70

The Greyhound Bus Incident
A Search for Justice
Compiled by
Sheriff James K. Jennings
September 2, 1983

I am composing this report to work
through the remorse I feel over the
deaths of Thomas O'Claire and his wife,
Alice, whom I shot outside Spratling
Manor, leaving their infant son, William,
an orphan.

1958
Julius Spratling had a problem with his
only child, his daughter, Gerda. At age

twenty-two the woman had no romantic
prospects and, being considered somewhat
homely, seemed doomed to live out her
days as a spinster.

In an attempt to pacify his daughter,
Julius Spratling hired a suitor: a cocky
young custodian from his factory named
Clint Eberhart.

Mr. Eberhart loved to flirt with the
factory girls, often inviting them to
join him for makeout sessions in an
abandoned machine shop behind the
factory.

Julius Spratling offered Mr. Eberhart a
lucrative payday if he married Gerda. Mr.
Eberhart agreed but failed to mention to
Mr. Spratling that he was, in fact,
already married.

Eberhart proposed to Gerda and their
engagement was announced in all the local
papers.

On the afternoon of June 21, 1958, a
butler summoned Mr. Spratling to the
telephone for a call from Sister Elizabeth
Synnott. The nun ran a home for women in
need in Middleford, Massachusetts. One of
her residents had seen the engagement
announcement in the newspaper and claimed
that Clint Eberhart was her husband, who

had abandoned her several months earlier, leaving her poor and destitute. She then told the nun that she was pregnant with Mr. Eberhart's child.

Sister Elizabeth knew the girl named Mary making this accusation to be honest and trustworthy. She informed Mr. Spratling that she would publicly protest the upcoming nuptials.

Mr. Spratling challenged her. "Prove it," he said. "Let this girl make these slanderous allegations to my face!"

Sister Elizabeth advised him that Mary (O'Claire) Eberhart would be coming down to North Chester on the next bus. She and two of her colleagues would serve as chaperones for the frightened young woman.

Mr. Spratling confronted Mr. Eberhart with this news. The fact that Mr. Eberhart was already married didn't seem to trouble Mr. Spratling. The butler heard him declare, "I don't care about that! A deal is a deal! Clean up your mess. You will marry my daughter, but first you must get rid of this other woman!"

Eberhart caught up to the bus when it made its regular stop at a filling station near Crawford. While several

passengers boarded, Mr. Eberhart searched
for Mary. When he saw where she was
seated, he began to pound on her window
and cursed her for trying to rob him of
his "biggest paycheck ever."

Six members of the United States Army
who were passengers on the bus chased
Eberhart away.

Mr. Eberhart, however, did not give up.
He pursued the bus in his convertible.

At this point, the bus driver used a
two-way radio to make an urgent request
for help. A Connecticut State Police
motorcycle officer responded to the call.

Meanwhile, Mr. Eberhart took a shortcut
to the intersection of Route 13 and
Highway 31, where he presumably planned
to force the bus to a stop so he could
board it and "take care" of Mary. A
charred swing-blade knife was found in
the wreckage of his vehicle.

The motorcycle cop arrived at the
crossroads first.

When Mr. Eberhart saw the police officer,
he apparently changed his plan. No longer
content to stop the bus, he drove toward
the intersection in a manner clearly
intended to run the Greyhound off the road.

Officer Mulgrew was hit by Eberhart's

speeding vehicle, fell face-first to the pavement, and became trapped underneath the chassis as the Thunderbird sped toward the bus in the crossroads.

However, after hitting the police officer and then the bus, Eberhart lost control of his own vehicle. His car flew up into the forest, where it plowed into a massive oak tree.

According to an eyewitness, the bus slid off the highway and came to rest in a cornfield, where it exploded like a "galdern ball of fire."

The eyewitness put the time of death "for all them folks on the bus" at ten minutes before ten, "give or take a minute or two."

Mary (O'Claire) Eberhart was the only survivor.

CONCLUSIONS

Miss O'Claire (she understandably reverted to her maiden name after the incident) first told me about these events when I went to offer her condolences on the death of her son, Thomas, the young man I shot outside Spratling Manor.

I told her I was sorry for what I had

done. Much to my surprise, Miss O'Claire
said it was all her fault.

Apparently, she had decided in June of
1983 (on the twenty-fifth anniversary of
the Greyhound bus tragedy) to tell her
son for the first time what his father
(Mr. Clint Eberhart) had done.

Mary's revelations had the unintended
consequence of making Tommy covet the
money Julius Spratling had promised
Eberhart. He figured that as Eberhart's
only surviving heir, he was entitled to
payment for the services his father
performed back in 1958.

As you know, Mr. Spratling, you did not
see matters the same way.

When Tommy threatened to disclose your
long-buried secrets, you called the
police and demanded that we take care of
the situation. You claimed you were being
blackmailed.

In truth, you knew Mary O'Claire was a
recluse who would never tell anybody what
you and Eberhart had conspired to do. Her
son and his wife were your final threats.
No wonder you were so pleased when I
killed them both.

Shame on you, sir.

Their blood and the blood of all
Eberhart's victims is on your hands.

At that point in the narrative, the type changed color.
It was no longer a blurry carbon copy but a black-ink
original.

ADDENDUM

Yesterday, at eight p.m., I presented the
original of this report to Mr. Julius
Spratling. He told me he would read it.
　Apparently, he did.
　Last night, Mr. Spratling committed
suicide.
　I see no need to publicly tarnish the
Spratling name or to reveal what I know
to his only survivor, his daughter,
Gerda, a woman who has spent so many
years mourning the death of her "beloved"
fiancé, perpetuating the lie initiated by
her father.
　Therefore, my report shall remain
unpublished. The dead have been avenged.
It is time for the living to move on.
　I would, however, like to acknowledge
those who helped me compile this report.
　First, Ms. Mary O'Claire. It took a
great deal of courage for her to relive
that terrifying night.

249

I would also like to thank the newspaper reporters, the former Spratling Clockworks employees, the Greyhound bus personnel, the North Chester Public Library, and all those who helped me piece together the truth from 1958.

Finally, I would like to thank Mr. David Wilcox. As a young boy of ten, he was at the crossroads that night. This is the first time he has told anyone what he witnessed. In 1958, no one thought to ask the young boy any questions. After he read about the shootings of Tommy and Alice, he came forward to tell me everything he remembered about the original incident. I'm glad he did. If it wasn't for Mr. Wilcox's eyewitness account, we might never have known what actually happened at the crossroads.

71

"We should talk to Mr. Wilcox," said Judy. "If he was ten back in 1958, he'd be only what now? Sixty?"

"I'm afraid that might prove somewhat difficult," said Mrs. Emerson.

"There's a Wilcox family that lives close to our house. Their son plays with my stepson. Maybe they're related."

"Unfortunately, this particular Wilcox passed away a few years back. Tractor accident. He was a farmer. In fact, he owned all the land on both sides of the highway near your home. Rocky Hill Farms? That's what Davy Wilcox called his place."

"Davy?"

"Yes."

"What about Davy's father?"

"Oh, he died ages ago. I remember meeting him

when I was a child. A man of very few words, he always wore this Huckleberry Finn straw hat. . . ."

Judy stood up from the table. "I have to go home."

"Is something wrong, dear?"

"Yes. Davy Wilcox is my stepson's best friend. And— he's only ten!"

Zack pulled the blue tarp off the stump.

The kerosene fumes that had been trapped underneath flew up and seared his nostrils.

"Wow! That stinks!" He fanned the air with his baseball cap.

"Yep," said Davy. "Like a gas jockey's grimy green jumpsuit!"

The holes sunk into the stump were full of kerosene. There were three ten-pound sacks of charcoal leaning against the trees under the tree house and one propane grill hidden in the shrubs off to the side.

"The other fellers help out with the charcoal?" Davy asked.

"Yeah."

"Say, Zack?"

"Yeah?"

Davy pointed to the rolling grill with its attached white tank. "What's that?"

"One of the guys' fathers doesn't use charcoal, so he dragged their gas grill all the way over here."

"What the blazes was he thinking?"

"I dunno. I guess he figured a grill's a grill."

"About as sharp as a bowling ball, ain't he?"

"Yeah." Zack laughed as he dumped the first dusty bag of briquettes over the stump.

It felt good to laugh. He didn't care whether his dead mother saw him having fun: Davy Wilcox was the best friend he had ever had in his whole life.

73

The priest parked his Lincoln Town Car in front of Spratling Manor.

Sharon met him under the sagging portico. She held a flickering candle.

"Miss Spratling is waiting in the chapel. She apologizes for not sending her chauffeur to pick you up, but Mr. Willoughby is otherwise engaged."

Sharon led the priest down twisting corridors to the library and took him to a mahogany wall panel set between two towering bookcases.

"This way."

She pressed against the wall and a secret door slid open. The priest ducked his head and followed Sharon down the dark tunnel. Up ahead, he could see the fluttering light of more candles.

They neared the Spratling family chapel.

Tonight the priest would say prayers for Clint Eberhart, whose soul had departed this earthly realm fifty years ago this very night.

Or so the priest had been told.

Zack pushed the button on his watch to illuminate the dial.

"It's 9:52," he said. "Just like the clock in the tower, hunh?"

"Yep," Davy said. "Light her up!"

Zack held the box of matches.

"You do it," he said.

"What?"

"You light it. I'm afraid."

"Afraid of what, pardner?"

"I dunno. What if the stump explodes or something?"

"Kerosene don't explode. You're thinkin' gasoline."

"You do it! Okay? Please?"

Davy shook his head. "Nope. It's up to you. You're the chosen one, Zack."

"Me? Why?"

"Because this was too important to trust to anybody else. Light the match, Zack. It's time."

"What do I tell Judy when she—"

"We'll worry about that later. Light 'er up!"

Zack's hands were shaking so much he rattled the matchbox. He finally worked the lid open, pulled out a wooden Blue Tip, and scratched it along the strike pad. The match sparked but wouldn't light.

"Try again," urged Davy.

Zack snapped the match sharp and quick. The head flared to life and he flicked it at the stump. A small spot of blue flame erupted on the edge of a single clump of charcoal. Fire spread slowly at first, creeping across the briquettes, then—*whump!* The flames found the fuel-soaked wood.

"We're in business!" said Davy.

"Yeah." Zack brought his arm up to shield his face from the fire's intense heat. "You think we poured in too much kerosene?"

"Nah. It'll settle down."

A bell rang in the distance.

"Oh, no! Is that your father?"

"Dang. I reckon he finally figured out that we didn't follow him home. I'll go deal with him. You stay here."

"What?"

"See you later, Zack. And thank you. Thank you kindly."

"For what?"

"Doin' what needed to be done." Davy ran down the hill to the highway.

"Wait!" Zack heard the fire roar behind him, heard a hiss when it boiled what little water remained inside the old lady's flower bucket. The white cross's knotty wood popped like corn in the microwave.

"Davy?"

The flames shot higher and filled the black sky with burning red stars.

"Davy!"

No one answered.

Davy was gone.

75

"Oh, my."

The priest had never been inside the chapel before. It was a smallish room with four wooden pews facing a marble altar.

Gerda Spratling knelt in the front pew, dressed in a flowing white gown, her head covered by a bridal veil. A rack of fifty ruby votive candles flickered in front of her. But what amazed the priest most were the other statues.

Dozens of them. Maybe a hundred. Some were tiny. Others towered to six feet. They were everywhere. Standing on pedestals. Tucked into alcoves. All were carved to look like a handsome young man with slicked-back hair and bright blue eyes.

"Oh, my," the priest mumbled again. He thought this must be Miss Spratling's private shrine to the young Elvis Presley.

"That's my Clint," Gerda said, standing up from her cushioned kneeler. "The soul for whom we pray this night."

Father Murphy reached for his handkerchief, dabbed at his damp brow.

"Clint was my fiancé," Miss Spratling said. "I remain his eternal bride!"

The priest sponged more sweat. "How lovely."

"Sharon?" Miss Spratling called out. "Get on your knees. Clint needs your prayers, too. Tonight he needs all our prayers!"

76

Judy raced up Main Street.

She passed the town clock tower, still stuck at 9:52.

Ten minutes before ten, give or take a minute or two.

That was what Davy Wilcox had told Grandpa he'd seen. Back when he was a boy. Back when he was still alive.

Judy checked the dashboard clock.

10:10 p.m.

She couldn't believe what a terrible stepmother she was: She had sent Zack on a sleepover date with dead people.

77

The burning stump exploded into a shower of sparks, which landed like a cannon blast on the plywood deck of the boys' pirate ship.

The tree fort crackled with fire.

Zipper barked.

"You're right. We need Davy." Zack wove his way through the trees, down the slope to the highway. Zipper ran after him.

"There he is. See? In the cornfield." The fire was now so bright it cast long, jagged shards of light all the way across the highway. "Davy?"

Zack's best friend was fifty—maybe a hundred—yards away, but Zack could see him.

"Davy? You gotta come back! The fire's out of control!"

In the distance, Davy turned slowly.

"Hurry! It's burning down the tree fort!"

Davy waved.

And then he disappeared. He didn't walk into the wall of cornstalks or hide behind a tree—he *disappeared*!

Zack stood frozen in shock.

He had never battled an out-of-control fire before.

He had never seen his best friend vanish into thin air, either.

78

In the middle of the prayers, Miss Spratling sprang up.

"Do you hear that?"

"Hear what?" the priest asked.

"That horrible screaming!"

The priest looked insulted. "I was singing a hymn, Miss Spratling."

Miss Spratling ignored him and hurried from the chapel—desperate to silence the screaming no one else could even hear.

Davy was gone and the whole forest was about to burn down unless Zack did something fast.

He could run up to the house and roll out the garden hose. He could go into the garage and turn on the lawn sprinklers. He could run inside and grab a fire extinguisher.

Before he could decide what to do or where to run, the wind whipped up and sent another shower of sparks spewing out of the stump like an angry volcano. Now there were twenty small fires licking up the sides of trees, wilting the underbrush, heading for the house!

Some sparks landed close to the propane grill and a river of fire snaked its way toward the ten-gallon gas tank hanging off the side.

"Run, Zipper!" Zack screamed. "It's gonna explode!" He quickly scooped up his dog and dashed down the hill to the highway. When he reached the road, he kept running and headed for the graveyard. He had been safe there once before. He'd go there again and hide.

Hide from Dad and Judy and the firemen and—

The propane tank exploded.

Behind him, Zack heard metal ripping through the trees.

In a flash, the fire leapt out of the forest and shot across the backyard and started gorging itself on the house.

Zack cowered behind a headstone. The sky over his house was glowing a bright orange. Explosions shook the ground. The fire had found the gasoline-powered lawn equipment in the garage.

Zack Jennings had never been in bigger trouble. He had burned down his father's house. He might burn down the whole neighborhood.

He saw Judy's car driving down Route 13. She was on her way home.

And she used to like me. I think she really did.

Zack was ready to run away from home forever; he just didn't know where to go or which way to run.

"Finish the job," hissed a voice behind him.

It was the skinny preacher. The scary Bible campers were lined up behind him, but this time, they all looked pale and Zack could see blue veins rippling across their faces.

"Finish the job!" the children chanted, moving closer.

The preacher thumped his Bible. "Finish the job!"

Zack had to flee the graveyard before the ghosts grabbed him!

"Come on, Zip!"

They raced back down the hill to the highway and an old-fashioned convertible materialized out of the haze beneath the blinking stoplight in the crossroads.

The phantom car flew out of a smoky cloud and skidded to a stop. It appeared exactly the same way Davy had disappeared.

So did the shadow man.

The man with wavy hair who Zack had first seen slinking through his backyard on the night of the big storm. The shadow man stared up into the woods like he was searching for something, but all he found was fire.

"No!" Zack heard him scream before the man doubled over and clutched his belt like someone had just socked him in the gut. "Who did this to me?"

Zipper barked. The shadow man turned, saw them.

"You!" The man held his side and limped up the highway.

Zipper snarled, then dashed straight at the shadow man.

"Zipper!" Zack yelled. "Don't! Come back here!"

Zipper didn't listen; he nipped at the shadow man's ankles.

"Stupid dog! I'll cut off your ears!" The shadow man pulled out a knife and slashed at the air, but his wild flailing didn't scare Zipper, who kept lunging at his rolled-up pants cuffs.

"Zipper!" Zack heard sirens and blaring air horns as fire trucks raced up the road from town.

"Finish the job!"

The preacher and the creepy Bible campers were stumbling down the hill from the cemetery. Beyond them, behind the wrought iron fence, Zack saw other people he didn't recognize. Dead people.

"I'll get you, boy!" the shadow man screamed.

Zack was surrounded.

"Get in."

He whipped around and saw the old lady's Cadillac idling in the middle of the highway. The chauffeur leaned out his window.

"Get in, boy. Now!"

The rear window scrolled down.

"Hop in, dearie," the old lady said from the back-seat, trying hard to smile. "We're your only hope. It appears that demon spirits everywhere are crawling out of their graves to get at you!"

"No," Zack said.

"You shouldn't have torched my stump, kid!" Up the highway, the greasy-haired ghoul was limping toward them. "You're a Jennings, ain't you, boy? You and me got unfinished business!"

"Get in the car, boy!" said the old driver. "Hurry!"

Far in the distance Zack saw Judy reeling around underneath the blinking red beacon.

"Zack?" she cried out. "Where are you? Zack! Zack!"
She sounded mad.

Madder than my real mom ever got.

Zack ran to the Cadillac. It seemed his only choice.
He had to run away. The old lady had a car.

Miss Spratling yanked the door shut behind him.
"Mr. Willoughby? Drive!"

The chauffeur piloted the car down the center of the
highway. When they reached the crossroads, the man
with the slicked-back hair was gone. Zipper looked fine.
A little dazed and confused, but fine.

"My, my, my—isn't that your stepmother?" the old
lady whispered. "Does she know how much you like to
play with matches?"

Zack slid down so Judy couldn't see him but he could
see her.

She was crying.

She isn't mad. She's crying!

Zack sprang up.

"Be still, boy!"

Zack went to pound on the tinted window, but the
old woman caught his arm.

"I said be still!"

"Let me out, you old witch!"

Zack tugged on the door handle. It wouldn't budge.

"Let me out!"

"I will do no such thing. You, young man, must now
pay for the sins of your fathers!"

80

Judy's legs quaked. She couldn't find Zack. Her new house was burning down. George was on the other side of the globe. Gerda Spratling's creepy old Cadillac had just cruised up the road. She heard sirens. Fire trucks. Police.

And Zipper kept barking at her.

"What is it?"

Zipper ran up the road about twenty yards, stopped, and turned around. Barked.

"You want me to follow you?"

Zipper barked what had to be a "yes" and flew up the highway toward the graveyard. Judy followed. They ran all the way to the cemetery. Zipper barked louder, stood up on his hind legs, tried to scale the fence. Judy saw a baseball cap stuck on top of a railing. Zack's Mets cap!

She understood.

Zack had been in the graveyard again. Why? Maybe a dead farmer named Davy had lured him there.

No. Davy didn't want to hurt Zack. If he wanted to do that, he would have done it days ago.

Maybe Zack came here to hide, like he did the other night when the plumber was after them.

Okay. But hide from whom?

What if Zack was the one who started the fire? Then he'd be hiding from me!

She looked back toward the house. The firefighters were spraying water on the house, the garage, and that big stump in the backyard.

Looks like he destroyed Miss Spratling's descanso, too. . . .

The creepy old Cadillac!

"Judy?" Sheriff Hargrove came hiking up the cemetery hill behind her.

"We need to talk to Zack," he said.

"She has him!"

"Who?"

"Gerda Spratling."

"I'm afraid Miss Spratling has stepped out," Sharon said to the crowd gathered outside the door.

"We know," Judy said. "She stepped out to kidnap my son!"

Judy hadn't called George. Not yet. What good would it do? She was the one who had to find Zack. Fast.

"We'd like to look around," Hargrove said to Sharon.

"What is all this commotion?"

Gerda Spratling, dressed in her gauzy wedding gown, waltzed into the foyer.

Zipper barked.

"Kindly remove that vile creature from these premises."

"The dog stays," said Hargrove. "We need him to help us search your house."

"Tonight?"

"Yes, ma'am."

"Am I allowed to ask why?"

"My stepson is missing!"

"Really? Did you misplace him, dearie? My, my, my. How careless."

"Miss Spratling?" said Hargrove. "We need to search your house. We need to do so immediately."

"I saw you," Judy said to Spratling. "I saw your car."

"Where?"

"In the crossroads. You were there tonight!"

"Of course I was, dearie. I heard some young pyromaniac was attempting to destroy my roadside memorial. Tell me, Sheriff Hargrove: Has the fire department done their duty?"

He nodded. "The fire has been contained."

"Wonderful. Now, then, if you will excuse me . . ."

"Miss Spratling?" said the sheriff. "Maybe you didn't hear me. We need to search your house."

"Oh, I heard you, Sheriff Hargrove. However, I don't recall hearing you say you had a warrant. Did my dear friend Judge Brockman sign the appropriate papers?"

"Not yet, but he will."

"Come back when he does. Good night, all."

When she was certain Miss Spratling had gone to bed, Sharon hurried down the winding cobblestone path to the carriage house.

She couldn't sleep, not without checking in on her son. All the talk about the missing boy had scared her.

"What is it now?" her mother grumbled when she opened the door.

"I just wanted to be sure Aidan was okay."

"Aidan? He's not here. Mr. Willoughby picked him up hours ago."

"What?"

"He said Miss Spratling had given permission for Aidan to sleep up at the manor house tonight."

Zack had no idea where he was.

The room was dark and smelled wet—like a basement when it rained.

The old lady, assisted by the even older driver, had tied his hands behind his back with duct tape. Then the old man had looped a heavy bicycle chain through his arms and locked him to some sort of metal pole. The floor he was sitting on was cold and hard.

And the baby was crying.

"Don't worry, little guy," Zack whispered. "We're going to be okay. I promise."

The baby gurgled. Zack could see a half-empty bottle jammed into the padding of his portable car seat. The baby started kicking. Ready to scream again.

"Hey, have you ever seen the town clock?"

The baby cooed.

"Did you know there used to be monkeys and squirrels inside that clock tower?"

The baby arched his eyebrows.

"Yeah. They'd climb up the gear teeth to get to the nuts up top."

Zack made a funny face and wiggled his cheeks like he was washing walnuts. The baby giggled. He probably didn't understand a word Zack was saying, but he seemed to like the silly faces.

"Stop that!"

The old lady and her driver were back. She stormed into the room, bent over the baby.

The baby started bawling.

"Go ahead. Scream, child. Scream! It's good for the lungs. Helps them grow big and strong." Miss Spratling turned to Zack. "Clint will be back soon to finish his unfinished business with you. He'd be here now, but you weakened him. Oh, yes, you did. Your little campfire? That sapped his strength. But he'll be back. Tonight, dearie."

"Miss Spratling?" The old man tottered forward. "The police will be coming back, as well."

"Who cares? They'll never find you, boy. Never, ever, never. Clint's going to slice you up into tiny little pieces and all the king's horses and all the king's men won't be able to put you back together again!"

Zack knew he was in *huge* trouble: The old lady was insane, nuttier than Grandpa's clock tower!

"My beau, Clint, is quite angry at you, Mr. Jennings. Your petty pyrotechnic display has presented us with quite a problem. Before what's left of his tree withers and dies, his soul must take up residence in another vessel."

The old lady bent down to tell Zack her secret. "But guess what?" Her breath was hot and foul, her eyes wide. "Clint can live again! We don't need the oak tree! All his soul needs to do is crawl inside a body that carries his royal blood!"

The old lady leaned even closer. "His grandson? The plumber? That boy was handsome, but a weakling. He couldn't handle Clint's surging energy." Miss Spratling gazed at the baby. "But this son of his grandson? Why, Clint will slide inside this child with the greatest of ease! He will live again! He will grow up and marry me!"

"Miss Spratling?" The chauffeur tried again. "The police?"

"Yes, yes." Miss Spratling stroked Zack's chin. "Do you know why Clint's soul was allowed to linger so long on earth, dear boy? Because *I* built that memorial and prayed for him. Yes, I did. Every day for fifty years! Now, tell me, child: When you're dead and gone, who will pray to save *your* immortal soul? Will anybody even miss you? Will anybody care?"

Zack pulled back, banged his head against the pole.

"No. I think not. You burned down their house. They won't miss you at all!"

She cackled and the two old people shuffled out the door.

But Zack knew they'd be coming back.

And they'd be bringing the ghost from the tree.

Time crept slowly.

The baby fell asleep. Zack was alone with his thoughts and they were darker than the starless sky outside the big windows.

Will anybody care?

He had to think about it.

When Zack died, his father might be sad for a little while. Then he'd get busy like he always did. He'd pull himself together, focus on work, and "move on with his life"—just like he had when Zack's mother died.

Maybe he and Judy would have some kids of their own. Not right away. But in a year, maybe two. They'd have a son who didn't remind them so much of a dead wife.

His friends? Zack didn't have any. Just Davy, and he probably wasn't even real. What was he? A figment of Zack's overactive imagination? No. Judy saw him, too. The way Davy disappeared in the cornfield tonight, it was just like how the shadow man had appeared, the guy the old lady called Clint.

The guy who was a ghost.

Was Davy a ghost? Probably. The preacher and the

Bible camp kids in their old-fashioned clothes? Probably ghosts, too. Just like the Rowdy Army Men. Now that he thought about it, he realized that there sure seemed to be a lot of ghosts hanging around near the crossroads. Maybe Zack could join them. Maybe he could become the newest ghost kid haunting the highway.

Will anybody miss me?

Zipper? Did dogs miss people? Maybe. But only until somebody else filled their food bowl on a regular basis or slipped them a Whopper.

What about Judy?

Okay. Judy is different. Not just because she wore a purple wedding dress and is funny and likes to make up stories the same way I like to.

If I die, she might miss me.

She might really miss me!

83

"Back so soon?"

Gerda Spratling met the search party in the front hall. Ben Hargrove shoved the warrant under her nose.

"Mary Beth?" he said to the female officer restraining Zipper.

"I'm on it." The officer unclipped the dog's collar and let him loose.

"If that dog does his business on my rug . . ."

"Your house will smell a whole lot better." Judy couldn't resist.

Zipper raced up and down the hallways, darted in and out of rooms. The police officer followed.

"Got anything, boy?"

Zipper barked, as if to say "No. Nothing."

"We'll find him, Zip." She offered the dog some water from a kidney-shaped bottle she kept strapped to the back of her utility belt.

Zipper didn't drink any. He was too busy.

He needed to find his boy.

"My son is missing, too!" Sharon cornered Hargrove and Judy in the portrait gallery. "Miss Spratling sent her chauffeur down to the carriage house to steal him!"

"Where's this chauffeur now?" Hargrove asked.

"I don't know!" Sharon's voice was shaky.

Hargrove spoke into his walkie-talkie. "Betty?"

"Go ahead," a voice crackled back.

"We need to issue an APB for . . ." He turned to Sharon.

"Willoughby!" she screamed. "Rodman Willoughby!"

It was almost two a.m.

Judy doubled back to Miss Spratling's bedchamber in the mansion's massive library. Between bookcases, she noticed one wall panel was slightly larger than all the others. She pushed against it and the whole wall slid open.

"Hello?"

She walked down the dark corridor and into the chapel.

"Oh, my," she gasped when she saw all the statues.

"Handsome, isn't he?"

Miss Spratling was standing behind her in that yellowing bridal gown, a lacy cape draped across her withered shoulders.

"Where's Zack?" Judy demanded. "What have you done with my son?"

Miss Spratling ignored her, moved to another statue.

"Where did you take Zack, you old witch?"

"Such language? In a chapel?" Miss Spratling clucked her tongue. "Shame on you, Mrs. Jennings! Shame, shame, shame."

"Where is he?"

"Well, dearie, I imagine he is burning in hell!"

"Sheriff?" Judy yelled up the hallway. "She's in here!"

"Yes, I imagine he's down there paying for the sins of his hideous grandfather."

"You know what, Miss Spratling? Your father was right. You are ugly. Not your face—even though it does sort of look like a withered old apple. No. I'm talking about your soul. It's beyond ugly. It's hideous."

"How dare you speak that way to me!"

"I know how your father bought you a boyfriend."

"He did no such thing!"

"Yes, he did. He paid Clint Eberhart to be nice to you."

"Go! Leave here now!"

"Or what?"

"Judy?" Sheriff Hargrove came into the chapel.

"Officer! Arrest this woman! She is being verbally abusive!"

Judy smiled. "The truth hurts, doesn't it?"

"Arrest her this instant!"

"Judy?" Hargrove put his hand on Judy's shoulder. "Back off. She's not worth it."

"She has Zack."

"We found her; we'll find him. You've done enough."

Much to Miss Spratling's delight, Sheriff Hargrove took Judy's elbow and led her out of the chapel.

85

A young cop escorted Judy out of Spratling Manor.

"My vehicle's parked over this way, ma'am."

"Where are we going?"

"Sheriff Hargrove says you need to calm down. I'm taking you over to headquarters so you can, you know, calm down."

Calm down? Judy absolutely hated it when people said that to her. *And this guy said it twice.*

They headed toward the driveway. A dog started barking in the forest.

"That sounds like Zipper!" Judy said. "Maybe he found Zack!"

The officer reached for his walkie-talkie.

"Officer? Officer!" A boy they couldn't see called out from the trees.

"Yeah?" The young cop moved toward the dark thicket, unsnapped his holster.

"Down here! In the woods! Jiminy Christmas, this galdern dog smells something!"

Zipper barked louder. Judy knew who was hidden in the trees with him. Davy.

"Hurry, Officer!"

The cop turned to Judy. "Mrs. Jennings? Wait right here."

"Yes, sir."

The young cop stepped into the underbrush.

Judy gave him a ten-second head start. Waited for his flashlight to disappear behind the dense foliage. Then she took off. She ran across the lawn, found a pebbled path, and followed it downhill to the river and an old, sagging boathouse. She pushed the door open and heard water lapping against the pilings underneath the floorboards.

About two minutes later, she heard Zipper panting.

"Howdy, Mrs. J.," said Davy from the shadows. "I hope that galdern police officer don't find himself in too big a pickle. He sure did take off a runnin' when he heard old Zip, though, didn't he?"

"What do you mean she 'slipped away'?" Sheriff Hargrove yelled at his bumbling young deputy.

"Well, sir, I proceeded down through the sticker bushes to pursue and apprehend—"

"She's trying to escape!" Sharon came running out of the mansion. "Miss Spratling stole my car!"

"When?" asked Sheriff Hargrove.

"I don't know!"

"Then how do you know she's the one who stole it?"

"She dropped this!" Sharon held up an antique blue garter—the kind a bride might've worn fifty years ago. "It was right where I parked my car!"

Hargrove nodded. "What type of vehicle are we looking for, ma'am?"

"A silver Hyundai."

"Okay, everybody," Sheriff Hargrove barked to his troops. "Let's roll!"

"What about Mrs. Jennings?" asked the young deputy.

"We'll worry about Judy later. She couldn't have gone too far because she doesn't have a car!"

"You sure, Chief?"

"Yes, I'm sure! I drove her over here, didn't I?"

All the police officers climbed into their vehicles to chase after the one woman they knew *was* currently driving a car: Miss Gerda Spratling.

86

"Davy?" Judy asked. "Where's Zack?"

"In a whole heap of trouble. We figure he might be up against ol' Clint Eberhart himself."

"The man who ran the bus off the road?"

"You done your homework, I see."

"Yeah. I usually do."

"Well, Eberhart is the sorriest soul you could ever meet. A black-haired devil . . ."

"With blue, blue eyes? Slicked-back hair?"

"That's the feller! You seen him?"

"No, no. So far I've only seen his statues."

"Statues?"

"Yeah. Tons of them."

"Dang. Where they at?"

"Inside the chapel."

"Chapel? Don't tell me Gerda Spratling built that dirty dog another dag-blasted memorial!"

"So it would seem, Davy."

"Well, Mrs. J., I reckon we need to burn that one down, too."

The old man shoved rusty gears to one side of the long table. Heavy cogwheels and hardware clanged and banged on the floor.

"A little quieter, if you please, Mr. Willoughby," Miss Spratling said as her loyal chauffeur cleared off the greasy workbench.

She moved to Zack. The boy was sitting on the cracked concrete floor, his wrists bound behind his back, his arms chained to the steel pole.

"I'll wager your stepmother has already forgotten you," she said with a dramatic sigh. "And your father? Why, he could care less. I'm told he's out of town on business, couldn't be bothered."

Zack didn't say anything. He was biding his time because he had a hunch about how to beat Clint Eberhart when he got there. It was an idea based on what

Davy Wilcox had taught him—actually, what Davy had *shown* him.

"Hey, Gerdy. What's shaking, doll?"

The ghost of Clint Eberhart limped into the room. He tried to smile, tried to swagger, but Zack could see he was wounded. Weak.

Miss Spratling's hand fluttered over her heart. "Are you all right, my love?"

"Yeah. But we need to hurry, doll."

"Yes, dear. Mr. Willoughby?"

Willoughby had the knives and saws spread out on the workbench.

"Put the kid up on the table, Gerdy."

"Mr. Willoughby? I will require your assistance."

"Hurry." Eberhart winced. He was getting weaker every second.

The old chauffeur groaned as he bent down to unlock the chain.

It was almost time. The lock snapped open.

Now!

Zack rolled sideways and cut the old man's legs out from under him. Willoughby toppled to the floor. Zack had used the rolling-tackle move before—playing Madden NFL on his PlayStation. It worked in real life, too.

Zack had been twisting at the duct tape binding his wrists, stretching it out while his hot sweat worked to dilute the glue. Now it was easy to slip free.

"Clint?" Miss Spratling cried. "Do something! Please?"

"Don't move, kid!" Eberhart screamed, but he didn't do anything.

Zack's theory was correct! Eberhart couldn't hurt him, couldn't touch him, couldn't *do* anything except make noise and order these two old farts around. Just like Davy Wilcox couldn't *do* anything. Davy never hammered a nail or drilled a hole or even ate a hamburger. Davy told Zack what to do and then stood around and watched Zack do it because Davy couldn't *do* anything.

"Don't let that kid—"

Eberhart groaned in agony. He doubled over and clutched his stomach.

"Clint? Sweetheart?"

"Accckkk . . ."

"Clint?"

Now Zack tore the tape off his legs.

Eberhart fell to his knees and slumped forward. But before his body hit the floor, he vanished into a swirling puff of dust.

Zack was getting used to these vanishing acts, so he didn't skip a beat to watch Eberhart vamoose into the vapor. He was up and ready to run. He could've gone straight for the door, could've saved himself, but he wanted to save the baby, too. So he ran back to the center of the big room to grab the handle on the Tote 'n Go car seat.

The old lady snagged him, wrapped her bony fingers tight around his wrist. Then she pressed a serrated knife blade against his throat.

"And just where do you think you're going, young man?"

88

"Smash the galdern windows, too!"

Judy had used candles to set the altar cloth on fire. She had thrown a dozen votives to the floor to start the carpet burning. Now the chapel was filling with toxic fumes, but Davy was right: There was still time to shatter the stained-glass windows and destroy a few more statues.

"This will weaken him?"

"You bet, Mrs. J. Ol' Clint Eberhart's probably clutchin' his gut right now and wonderin' why he feels so galdern weak!"

Zipper tore apart the velvet cushion in the front pew with his teeth: It still had Spratling's scent on it.

Judy slammed a statue through a stained-glass window. "You ever do any work, Davy?"

"Can't, I reckon. But I'm full of good ideas, ain't I?"

A bell chimed in the distance. "They want me back, Mrs. J."

"Tell me what I need to do."

"Can't do that, neither."

"Really? Who writes all these rules?"

"Folks upstairs. Frustratin', ain't it?"

Zipper snarled.

"What do you two think you're doing in here?"

Clint Eberhart grasped a marble pedestal and struggled to keep standing.

Judy looked at the statue in her hand. Looked at Eberhart. She slammed the statue against the hard edge of a pew.

"Hey! Lady! Easy!"

She banged it again. The blows struck Clint as if she were wielding a plaster voodoo doll.

"Put that thing down! Come on. Cut me some slack, doll."

Judy turned to Davy. "Is he a ghost, too?"

"Yes, ma'am."

Judy swung the statue she was holding like a baseball bat at the knees of another statue. Eberhart crumpled to the floor.

"Stop! Ouch! That hurts!"

Judy hacked a cough. She was inhaling too much smoke. Currently, Judy and Zipper were the only two creatures in the room who actually needed to breathe. Therefore, they also needed to leave.

"Davy?" Judy peered through the haze. It stung her eyes. "We need to get out. Now."

Davy didn't answer.

He'd disappeared.

It was just Judy, the dog, and the demon squirming on the floor.

She stood over him. Raised her statue high.

"Where's Zack?"

"Where you'll never find him!"

"Where?"

Eberhart moaned.

"Come on, Mrs. J.!" It was Davy. Somehow, he had transported himself out of the chapel and into the library at the other end of the secret passageway. "You best get out before the fire gets you!"

Eberhart struggled to his feet. "Where's your son?" he snarled. "On his way to hell!"

Judy turned. "Which way, Davy?"

The boy was gone. Again.

"Come on, Zipper! Run!"

They had at best a ten-step lead.

And no one left to help them.

Gerda Spratling was on her knees, ferociously praying to revive Eberhart's wounded soul.

The baby kicked and screamed.

"Miss Spratling?" Willoughby held his head. "The baby?"

Miss Spratling kept mumbling prayers.

"They're going to arrest you, too," Zack said to Willoughby. He was chained to the pipe again. "Accessory to murder, I figure."

"Be quiet!"

"They'll probably give you one of those lethal-injection deals."

"Miss Spratling?"

"You know how they do that? Well, they have this *huge* needle," Zack said. "I hear it's like three or four feet long."

"Miss Spratling?"

"They stick that needle in your butt."

"Miss Spratling!"

The baby screeched.

"And that needle's full of rat poison."

"Miss Spratling?"

The baby sent his bottle skidding across the floor and let loose a squeal. Willoughby lunged toward Spratling and shook her.

"Miss Spratling!"

"How dare you interrupt my prayers!"

"I can't do this! I can't!"

"Pray with me, Mr. Willoughby." Her right hand disappeared under the folds of her gown.

"I don't want to die from a lethal injection!" He shambled over to the pole, fumbled in his pocket for the keys.

"Rodman?"

The old chauffeur undid the lock behind Zack's back.

"What do you think you're doing?"

"What I should have done ages ago: say no to one of you miserable Spratlings!"

"Mr. Willoughby? Are you forgetting certain documents I keep locked in Father's safe?"

"I don't give two hoots about it anymore! I'm old! I have no children! Who cares if you blackmail me?"

While the old folks argued, Zack slowly slid across the floor . . . easing over to . . . the baby . . . the portable car seat. . . .

"Why, you ungrateful, insolent old man!"

Miss Spratling reared up. The knife blade came out from under her wedding gown and glinted over her head.

"Don't do it!" yelled Zack. He grabbed the handle on the baby seat. "Leave Mr. Willoughby alone or I swear I'll take this baby so far away, you and your boyfriend will never find him!"

"Hah! You wouldn't get far! I'd catch you!"

"Really? And just how fast can you run in that wedding dress?"

The old lady slowly lowered the knife but kept it aimed at Mr. Willoughby's heart. "Fine. We'll simply wait for Clint to return. He'll deal with you," she sneered. "He'll deal with you both!"

Judy and Zipper raced back into the mansion's library.

Davy had disappeared again and so had Eberhart. But it seemed some other tormented spirit was in the room with them because Judy heard ghostly moaning from somewhere up near the ceiling.

Zipper ran over to the rolling ladder attached to the towering bookcases.

"Hello?" Judy called out. She saw the faint outline of a man standing near the top of the ladder. "Who are you?"

The man held a sputtering candle. He turned slowly and looked down.

Judy recognized the man because she had seen his face in the old newspaper clippings: Julius Spratling. Gerda's dead father. He was dressed in a dark blue business suit. There was an anguished look on his waxy face.

He blew out the candle and something fluttered

through the air: a glowing square of soft light, a phantom sheet of paper. It drifted down lazily like a tumbling leaf. When it finally hit the library floor, it bounced up half an inch and slid underneath one of the massive bookcases.

Judy hurried over to where the thin rectangle of light had disappeared. She bent down and saw an ancient binder. It was covered by almost an inch of dust.

Was it the report from the safe-deposit box?

She reached in. Grabbed the slender book. Read its cover.

```
The Greyhound Bus Incident
   A Search for Justice
```

Yes! It was the same report. Only this wasn't a carbon copy. This had to be the original Grandpa Jennings had presented to Julius Spratling on the night he committed suicide. The pages were yellowed. The plastic spine had faded. It had, apparently, been hidden under the bookcase for the past twenty-five years.

Judy slowly opened the booklet and the pages began to flick forward—all by themselves! The flipping paper came to a sudden stop when it reached a page where certain words, down near the bottom, seemed to glow with an eerie light.

```
Mr. Eberhart loved to flirt with the
factory girls, often inviting them to
```

join him for makeout sessions in an abandoned machine shop behind the factory.

The machine shop. Behind the factory.
That's where they took Zack!
"Come on, Zipper. We have to hurry!"
Judy looked up to thank Mr. Spratling.
She saw his ghostly body swinging at the noosed end of a tasseled rope.

Judy and Zipper raced out of the library and were blinded by a brilliant white light.
"Davy?"
Clint Eberhart stumbled into the dusty beam. "That hillbilly beaned me with his slingshot!"
While Eberhart rubbed his ear, Judy and Zipper took off.
They both knew the way to the front door because they had been up and down this corridor all night long. Now they needed to outrun the limping hellion and go rescue Zack at the abandoned Spratling Clockworks Factory.
But how are you going to get there?
The factory was a good fifteen-minute drive from Spratling Manor.
You don't have a car. Remember? You came over here with Sheriff Hargrove.

"You think you can run away, dolly?"

Eberhart was gaining on them.

Judy would ponder her transportation problems later. Right now she needed to run. She followed Zipper around a corner and saw moonlight leaking in around the front doorjamb. If they could make it outside, they might have a chance.

"Thought I'd have to settle for killing your boy. Now I get to kill you and his dog, too!"

"Faster, Zipper!" They raced to the front door, yanked it open, and then slammed it shut behind them. Judy couldn't tell who was panting louder: her or the dog.

"Hey there."

She turned around. Billy O'Claire was standing on the porch. He looked paler than usual.

"That toilet upstairs still giving you trouble?"

"N-no," Judy stammered, and tried not to stare at the ghost she had actually known when he was alive. "Our house burned down."

"Well, that's one way to fix your plumbing problems. Oh, I'm supposed to tell you to borrow the old lady's car. It's around back. A Caddy. The keys are in the ignition."

"Noooo!" It was Eberhart, wailing on the other side of the front door.

"You better hurry before my grandfather figures out he can walk through walls."

"Thanks," said Judy.

"Hey, your son's taking care of my son. I figure it's the least I can do."

Judy and Zipper took off running and saw the Cadillac parked in the side driveway.

Zipper jumped through the open window and bounded over to the passenger seat, where he yapped at Judy to hurry up and drive! She pulled open the heavy door, climbed behind the steering wheel, and twisted the ignition. The antique auto, meticulously maintained by the chauffeur for five decades, started right up.

"Hang on," Judy said. She slipped the car into gear and pointed it toward the winding driveway that would lead them down to the front gates. Zipper stuck his head out the window and barked goodbye to Billy O'Claire as the plumber faded into the night.

Judy pressed down on the gas pedal.

Zipper cocked an ear.

Then Judy heard it, too: another car, revving its engine.

She checked the rearview mirror and saw Clint Eberhart behind the wheel of a 1958 Thunderbird convertible.

Great, she thought. *The car's a ghost, too!*

91

It was a standoff: Spratling had the knife; Zack had the baby.

The chauffeur stood trembling between them.

Miss Spratling stepped into a pool of cold moonlight. She rotated the knife in her gnarled fist. Its sharp edge glistened.

"Clint's coming," she hissed. "Do you hear him? Listen! He's riding here on the wind."

Zack heard the wind whistling through a broken-out windowpane.

"That's Clint," Miss Spratling insisted. "He's coming back to kill you and Mr. Willoughby."

Frightened, Willoughby braced himself against the pole.

"You should go, son," he said, nearly breathless. "Take the baby. Run away. Hurry! Before Mr. Eberhart returns."

"Don't worry, sir," said Zack. "Eberhart can't hurt us. He's a ghost. He can't do anything except try to scare us into hurting ourselves or giving *her* what she needs."

"Really?" said Miss Spratling. "Are you sure about that, Mr. Jennings? Clint is different. He was trapped inside that tree so long, he has acquired certain special powers."

Zack heard another window rattling behind him.

He whipped around to see if it was Eberhart launching some kind of sneak attack.

No. It was just a scraggly tree branch, buffeted by the wind, tapping its fingers against the dingy glass.

The old lady cackled. "What's the matter, boy? Afraid of trees?"

Zack spun back around. "No," he said. "Not anymore."

22

The Cadillac had an old-fashioned cell phone the size of a bread loaf. The chauffeur had probably installed it sometime in the late eighties, but it still worked. Judy called 911.

"Tell Sheriff Hargrove that Zack Jennings is being held at Spratling Clockworks. Out back in the machine shop."

She knew that the 911 operator would immediately send all available units screaming to the abandoned old factory. She didn't, however, mention the phantom convertible chasing after her as she and Zipper sped down Route 13 in Gerda Spratling's 1952 Cadillac Coupe DeVille.

Now Zack heard something else behind him: police sirens! The cavalry was coming!

Miss Spratling heard them, too.

"Back here!" Zack screamed. "Back here!"

"Zack?" yelled a voice, far off in the distance.

Zack, clutching that baby carrier, hurried over to the door.

"We're back here!"

He heard something metal hit the floor. He twirled around.

The old lady had dropped the knife and was getting away through the back door.

Zack wanted to chase after her, but he still had the baby and Mr. Willoughby to worry about.

"Back here!" he screamed. "Hurry!"

= = =

She got away!" Zack said when the police arrived two minutes later.

"Don't worry, Zack," said Sheriff Hargrove. "You did the right thing. Thanks to you, the baby is safe."

"She's in a silver Hyundai. The car that followed her to the crossroads every Monday! I saw her drive away!"

"Well, she won't get far. We'll catch her."

"Where's Judy?"

"We don't know, son."

"Is she safe?"

The sheriff shook his head. "We don't know that, either."

Gerda Spratling had learned to drive when she was sixteen.

However, with Mr. Willoughby constantly at her beck and call, she had not driven much in the intervening fifty-six years. Now she was hunched behind the wheel of Sharon's silver Hyundai, moving slowly. She was headed home to the manor because she sensed Clint would be there waiting for her.

Clint will know what to do!

Clint Eberhart's Thunderbird was gaining on Judy, so she gunned the Cadillac, jammed the accelerator all the way to the floor.

"Come on, ghost boy! Show me what you've got!"

She bounded up a knoll, left the pavement, and

landed with a rocking thud that sent Zipper's head bobbling like a dashboard dachshund.

There was a slow-moving vehicle blocking the road in front of them.

A silver Hyundai doing thirty-five miles per hour.

The Cadillac pulled up alongside the Hyundai.

Gerda Spratling saw Mrs. Jennings behind the wheel. "How dare she! That woman stole my automobile!"

The old lady stomped on the gas pedal with all the strength her surging hate could provide.

Judy saw the blinking red light where 13 crossed 31 and decided to barrel through the intersection to make Miss Spratling and Clint Eberhart chase after her. She'd lead them both away from the factory and Zack and out into the Connecticut countryside.

Maybe all the way to New Hampshire.

She looked both ways when she hit the crossroads but didn't even think about stopping.

Gerda Spratling squeezed the steering wheel, leaned forward, and willed the whining Hyundai to move faster.

Faster!

Then she saw a familiar figure standing at the edge of the crossroads and forgot all about catching up with George Jennings's wife.

It was Mary O'Claire.

The girl who told Sheriff Jennings all those lies! Claimed Clint was her husband. Hah!

The young woman stretched out her arms and beckoned Miss Spratling into the crossroads.

"Dirty, stinking, stupid liar!" Spratling aimed the car straight at the ghostly apparition.

Mary drifted to the right.

Spratling matched her move, cut her wheels sharply.

The little car was doing sixty miles per hour when it entered the crossroads. That sudden twist of the steering wheel caused it to flip over and tumble down the asphalt. When it finally stopped rolling, when the roof caved in and the gas tank ruptured, when it looked like a rusty beer can flattened under a truck tire—the car exploded.

95

Judy looked up at her rearview mirror and saw Miss Spratling swerve off the road.

Then she heard the explosion.

She eased onto her brakes, executed a U-turn, and drove back to where the small car had erupted into a fireball.

No way could Miss Spratling still be alive.

Zipper stood up in the passenger seat, his front paws planted firmly on the headrest so he could look out the rear window. He yipped and wagged his tail. The bad man was gone. The Thunderbird was nowhere to be seen.

Judy dialed 911 to report the accident.

"Your name?" the operator asked.

"Judy Magruder Jennings."

"Mrs. Jennings? Sheriff Hargrove said if you called, I

should tell you Zack is fine. Apparently, he was also very brave."

"Is that so?"

"That's what Ben told me. Said your son is a hero, saved a baby's and an elderly gentleman's lives tonight."

The operator informed Judy that a fire truck and an ambulance were on their way to the crossroads. Judy hung up, climbed out of the car, and hurried toward the flaming wreck. She moved as close as she could until the heat forced her to step back. The fire department would have to handle the blazing wreck.

Judy needed to go see her son.

Zack and Judy spent the rest of the night at a Holiday Inn.

First thing the next morning, Judy called Mandica and Son Tree Service and asked them to "Please go rip out what's left of that stupid stump in our backyard."

Mr. Mandica thought it was an odd request—worrying about tidying up your yard when you didn't even really have much of a house anymore.

Judy offered to pay him double his usual price if he took care of the job, as she put it, *"today!"*

Sheriff Hargrove suggested that Judy keep the Cadillac for a little while since her own car had been badly damaged when the garage around it had burned down.

= = =

"This car is kind of creepy, hunh?" Judy said as they drove up Route 13.

"Yeah."

They were coming from dinner at Burger King. Judy had bought Zipper his own Double Whopper, no onions. She figured the dog had earned it, going up against the ghost of Clint Eberhart the way he had.

Now Zack and Zipper shared the front passenger seat. The dog burrowed in Zack's lap, enjoying his after-dinner nap.

"Don't worry," said Judy. "We'll buy a new car. We'll build a new house. Those kinds of things are easy to replace."

After waiting all day, Zack popped the big question: "So, any idea what I should tell Dad about the fire?"

"Don't worry. We'll think of something."

"We?"

"I should've listened to Bud and had that tree chopped down. So in a way the fire is my fault, too. I know—we'll tell your dad I was attempting to make toast again."

Zack laughed and it felt good.

"You know," said Judy, "I never really liked that house."

"What?"

"Seriously. Sure, it was huge, but it only had a break-fast nook. Where were we supposed to eat lunch? Our next house will definitely have that lunchroom."

"What about a detention hall in the hallway?"

"Nope." She tousled Zack's hair. "We don't need one. Nobody I know ever does anything really, really bad."

They reached the blinking light. Judy signaled for a left turn.

"I thought we were going back to the Holiday Inn."

"We are. I just want to check something."

She parked the Cadillac on the shoulder of the road in the same spot where Miss Spratling always parked it on Mondays.

"I want to make sure Mr. Mandica did a good job. Come on."

They left Zipper sleeping peacefully in the car and headed up into the trees.

In the darkness they could make out two new paths of raw clay cut through the underbrush: the result of a backhoe's heavy tank treads trampling down everything in their way. A huge crater was scooped into the rocky soil where the oak tree had once stood. The stump was gone.

"Wow," Zack said, staring into the gaping pit. "It must've had a ton of roots."

The hole was at least a dozen feet deep, twenty feet wide. Its sides were scraped clean.

"I think this tree was evil," Judy said. "I really do."

Zack nodded his agreement. "Yeah. Me too."

"Shoot." Judy saw something on the far side of the trench.

"What?"

"A root. See? Near the top? Call me crazy, but I want that thing outta here!"

Judy slid down the stony slope. Zack slid after her. They worked their way around to what had to be the last remnant of the towering tree. Judy grabbed hold of the muddy runner and yanked. It wouldn't budge.

"Let me help you." Zack scraped away dirt until he exposed enough root to give them good handgrips.

"On three," Zack said. He and Judy anchored their feet against the bank. "Ready? One, two—"

"What do you two think you're doing?"

They whipped around.

Eberhart.

He looked sickly. Feeble. But he was still there, teetering at the edge of the giant hole.

"Pull, Zack!" Judy shouted.

Eberhart schussed down the far side of the pit.

"Pull hard!" They yanked. The root was a long, craggy rope.

"Let go!" Eberhart moaned. "Leave me alone!"

The root started popping up through the topsoil.

"Keep pulling!" They leaned back, wrenched harder. The root kept snapping up, cutting a narrow furrow nine feet long.

"I'll kill you both!"

Finally, the last sinewy strands sprang free. Zack and Judy flew backward, slammed against the hard dirt wall behind them.

All they could hear was their own hard, steady breathing. Zack smelled something foul. Rotten eggs.

"P.U."

"Yeah," Judy said. "Sulphur. What they used to call brimstone."

"Look!" Zack pointed to a puddle of murky sewer water sizzling in the bottom of the pit. It looked like some kind of oily acid bath bubbling in a six-inch circle of sludge. Only the bubbles weren't popping up; they were being sucked down into the ground.

Judy and Zack crabbed up the slope as fast as they could. Their skittering feet sent pebbles and dirt showering down into the hole. When they made it to the crater's rim, Judy, her adrenaline pumping, flopped backward and stared up at the stars. She took in a deep breath and tried to stop her heart from leaping out of her chest.

"Wow," she said. "Okay. That was exciting. I think, you know, he's gone. Finally. For good. This is officially *over*. Mr. Eberhart won't be coming back. You know, I read this article once about how in olden days they used to bury their criminals near a crossroads so the ghosts of the damned wouldn't be able to find their way back into town, in case, you know, they ever rose up to seek revenge like Mr. Eberhart obviously—"

Zack nudged Judy. "Uh, Judy? I don't think it's over."

"Howdy, pardner! Mrs. J."

Davy Wilcox stood, hands on his hips, at the far side of the crater.

"Hey," Zack said.

"Hello, Davy," Judy said. "Good to see you again."

There was a noise behind Davy. A rustle of leaves. Three nuns stepped out from the shadows, their black habits fluttering in the breeze.

"You done good, Zack," Davy said. "Ripped out every inch of that galdern tree."

"Well, Judy helped."

"Bless you both," said Sister Elizabeth.

"Thanks, son," said a handsome man in what looked like an air force uniform.

"Davy?" Zack asked. "Who are all these people?"

"Well, them there are some real swell nuns. And that

feller in the snazzy uniform, that's Bud. He's the bus driver."

"That's the gentleman who helped me change my flat tire." Judy waved at Bud. Bud snapped her back a salute.

"We're behind schedule, folks," Bud said. "Time to board up."

Zack saw a pale blond girl dressed all in white.

"Davy?" Zack whispered. "That girl. She's a ghost, right?"

"Yep, but don't say nothin'. She don't even know she's dead—keeps trying to hitch a ride into town so she can go to a summer social!"

The crowd grew.

"I told 'em, Zack—said you were the man for the job!"

A locomotive beacon of light shone from the dead cornfield on the far side of the highway. Zack could see a silver Greyhound bus glowing from the inside out, as if it were a Japanese lantern and someone had jammed a five-hundred-billion-watt bulb inside it.

"Step lively, folks," the bus driver said as he marched down the hill.

Several passengers followed him across the highway and into the cornfield. In the crossroads, beneath the blinking stoplight, Zack saw a motorcycle cop acting like a school crossing guard.

"Say, now, where's the tree house?"

It was the aluminum-siding salesman.

"Move along, Mr. Billings," Davy said. Billings tipped his fedora and headed down the hill.

"Move along, children. Two by two. Move along."

Down in the road, Zack could see the scrawny preacher leading his Bible campers toward the light. Zack realized he had never seen any of the children smile before.

Now Zack saw six soldiers stumbling around in the cornfield. The Rowdy Army Men.

"Well, I reckon I best be going, too, pardner."

"Wait!" said Zack. "This is too weird. I just saw the Rowdy Army Men and those Bible campers and—"

"They're all the folks what died on account of that fool Eberhart in the flip-top Ford. But don't you worry. Ol' Clint is headin' out of town, too." He looked down into the pit. "Only I suspect he's headin' in the opposite direction."

A bell pealed in the distance.

"Wait," said Zack. "Where's everybody going?"

"Where they shoulda gone fifty years back. But they was marooned down here on account of the memorial."

"The tree? I don't understand. Do you, Judy?"

"Maybe. Sort of."

"Zack," Davy said, "some folks will tell you that ghosts walk this earth on account of their unfinished business. But these folks? They were stuck here on account of *someone else's* unfinished business."

"Who?"

"Miss Gerda Spratling."

"She, uh, left town, too," Judy offered. "I think she and Mr. Eberhart have been . . . reunited." She nodded toward the bottom of the pit. "Permanently."

"Good riddance to bad rubbish," said Davy. "She made the hour of his death so dadgum sacred, she made these other folks prisoners to it, too. Of course, me and my pops helped."

"How?" asked Zack.

"Her tree was on our land and Pops saw no harm in letting her decorate it up if it helped her grieve. Me? I let her keep at it all them years. I didn't know she was trapping souls with it until I checked in upstairs myself: Gerda Spratling couldn't move on, so neither could they."

Davy fixed his gaze on the intersection of Highway 31 and County Route 13.

"I figure when you come to a crossroads, you have a choice: right turn, left turn, straight ahead. Or you can just pull over to the side of the road and call it quits. But if you've got a good stretch of road up ahead and someone fun to travel it with, I say why stay stuck in a galdern ditch?"

"I knew you were a ghost!" Zack said. "Not at first, but I sort of figured it out."

Davy looked down at his arms and curled his fingers. "Don't feel like no ghost, though. Can you see through me?"

"Nope."

"Dang. I always figured you could see through 'em, you know?"

"Yeah. Me too."

"When I learned what was going on, I volunteered to come on back. Be a boy again. See what I could do to set things right."

"Why'd you pick me to help you?"

"You were the only one brave enough. Adults? Most can't even see ghosts and those that can just get scared."

"It's true," Judy said. "We do."

The distant bell tolled more deeply.

"Davy?"

"Yeah, pardner?"

"We were really friends, though, right? You weren't just pretending to make me help you with the stump?"

"Zack, I'll tell you true: You were the best buddy any feller could ever hope to have. Weren't no pretending on my part about that. No, sir. Cross my heart and hope to die."

Davy waved, turned, and walked down the hill to the highway. He wouldn't be riding on the bus with the others because he had not been one of its original passengers.

Instead, he headed for the crossroads, where he disappeared into the darkness between strobes from the blinking stoplight overhead.

The bus vanished, too. The cornfield was dark and empty again.

It was really over.

Everybody had moved on.

"Wow," said Zack. "How cool." Then he turned to Judy and smiled. "Thanks, Mom. Thanks for everything!"

Judy smiled, too, even though she felt like crying: That was the first time Zack had ever called her Mom.

She sure hoped it wouldn't be the last.

Thank You

To J.J., who is my Judy.

To R. Schuyler Hooke and everyone at Random House.

To Eric Myers, my agent, who found Zack and Judy such a wonderful home.

To Meredith Sue Willis and her fiction writing class at NYU, where I first workshopped this idea.

To librarians everywhere. They are the real Jeanette Emersons, who help us find the knowledge we need.

To Tiger Lilly, who is my Curiosity Cat.

CHRIS GRABENSTEIN is the Anthony Award–winning author of the adult titles *Tilt-a-Whirl, Mad Mouse,* and *Whack A Mole.* Apparently, he spends far too much time at amusement parks. Here's a tip learned the hard way: Never eat six hot dogs prior to riding a roller coaster. He used to write TV and radio commercials and has written for the Muppets.

Chris was born in Buffalo, New York, and moved to Chattanooga, Tennessee, when he was ten. After college, he moved to New York City with six suitcases and a typewriter to become an actor and a writer. For five years, he did improvisational comedy in a Greenwich Village theater with some of the city's funniest performers, including this one guy named Bruce Willis.

Currently, Chris and his wife, J.J., live in New York City with three cats and a dog named Fred, who starred in *Chitty Chitty Bang Bang* on Broadway. You can visit Chris (and Fred) at www.ChrisGrabenstein.com.

Turn the page for a sneak peek
at another Zack and Judy chiller,

THE HANGING HILL

1

There's this thing about ghosts: Once you've seen one, you can basically see them all.

At least the ones that want to be seen.

At the age of eleven, Zack Jennings was learning the rules of the spirit world pretty quickly. He'd only seen his first real-live (make that "real-dead") spook maybe a month or two ago. Now they seemed to be everywhere. When he went to summer camp in the middle of July, he met the boy who'd drowned in the lake.

Back in 1973.

When he hung out at the library, he occasionally saw this pudgy woman reading over people's shoulders because she couldn't flip the pages herself anymore, what with being dead and all.

His mother had always claimed that Zack had a hyperactive imagination, but even he couldn't make this stuff up. The ghosts he saw were as real as electricity, wind, and gravity—things nobody could see but everybody knew were there.

Some called being a Ghost Seer a gift. Well, if it was,

Zack figured it was like getting a paisley-and-plaid sweater for Christmas when what you really wanted was an iPod. Seven weeks after learning he could see spirits, Zack was already tired of being special.

Being special could wear a guy out.

On the first Saturday of August, as he stepped into the brightly lit breakfast room of the Marriott extended-stay hotel near North Chester, Connecticut, it happened once again: He saw an apparition lurking near a small table in the far corner of the room.

Zack could tell: This one was a demon.

Zack and his family—his dad, his new stepmom, and his dog—were currently residing at the hotel because their house had burned down when Zack had battled the evil spirit haunting the crossroads nearby. The fire had been Zack's fault, and his allowance would be docked for the damages until he turned twenty-one. After that, Zack's dad would probably do payroll deductions. And now, here Zack was, less than twenty feet away from yet another fiend, who probably wanted to destroy some other part of Zack's life when all Zack wanted to do was grab a bowl of cereal and maybe a banana from the breakfast buffet.

Zack had come down to the lobby on his own.

His dad, who didn't believe in ghosts anyway, had gone into New York City for weekend work at his office.

His stepmom, Judy, an author, was upstairs, busily working on last-minute rewrites to *Curiosity Cat,* a new musical, based on her children's books, that was about to have its world premiere at a theater called the Hanging Hill Playhouse.

His trusty dog, Zipper, was also upstairs—snoozing between the cushions of a very comfy hotel couch.

There were other people in the breakfast room, the same ones Zack saw most mornings: Divorced Guy, Moving Family, Vacationing Family, Businessman, Other Divorced Guy.

The ghost was new.

Zack could tell that the man sitting at the table in the far corner of the breakfast room was a ghost because he was wearing old-fashioned clothes—the kind convicts in chain gangs sometimes wore in the movies. *Old* movies.

The ghost was, or had been, a hulking giant with a serious scowl carved into his watermelon-sized head. He wore a denim prison jumpsuit, loosely laced work boots, and a tin hat that looked like an upside-down spaghetti strainer with electrical cables clamped to battery posts where its legs should have been.

He'd shown up sitting in his own chair: a colossal throne made out of thick planks of rough-hewn lumber. Wide, double-holed leather belts were buckled tight across his chest, arms, and legs.

Zack suddenly realized the guy was strapped into an electric chair, the thing they used fifty years ago to execute hard-core criminals on death row in the state penitentiary.

The giant caught Zack staring.

"Pssst! Hey, kid!"

Zack pretended not to see or hear the man.

"I know you can see and hear me, kid."

So much for pretending.

"Come here. Undo these belt buckles!"

Slowly, very slowly, Zack turned his back on the ghost so he could face the breakfast buffet and make like he was picking out a banana. Behind him, he heard the sizzling sputter of sparks. He smelled ozone, like when an electrical outlet short-circuits and scorches the toaster plug. Zack whipped around just in time to see the last zig of a lightning bolt zap and *zizz* off the big guy's metal cap. Smoke wafted up from his razored scalp.

"Where's the bank?" the man in the chair demanded.

Zack didn't answer.

"Used to be a bank right here. Connecticut Building and Loan. Biggest heist of my career." Watermelon Head grinned. His teeth were the color of coffee beans. "Happiest day of my life, kid. Good times."

Zack glanced guardedly around the room. Nobody else could see or hear the ghost reminiscing about his bygone days of glory.

"Come on! Undo these straps!"

Now one of the kids in the Moving Family, a girl about six, was gawking at Zack like he was nuts. He didn't blame her. He probably looked pretty crazy: frozen in place, staring across the room at an empty table, mouth hanging open.

"Be a pal, kid! I've been stuck in this chair since 1959."

Zack didn't budge.

"You deaf? I said turn me loose!"

Zack stayed where he was.

"Oh, I get it," the trapped beast snarled. "Some kind of tough guy, hunh?"

Zack shook his head and slid his black-rimmed glasses up the bridge of his nose. He was sort of short and kind of skinny and really didn't look all that tough, even when he took off the glasses.

"Do you know who I am, kid?"

Again, Zack shook his head while the girl, the normal kid, kept gawking at him.

"Folks called me Mad Dog Murphy on account of the fact that I went bonkers here at the bank. Killed six people. Two of 'em kids! So shake a leg and unbuckle these straps! You think I want to spend eternity sitting on my keester on top of Old Sparky?"

Now a second ghost materialized directly across the table from the angry giant lashed into his sizzle seat. A woman. Zack couldn't see her face, just the back of her curly hair.

"Doll face!" Mad Dog Murphy said with a sinister smile. "What're you doin' here?"

The woman didn't say a word.

"What? Forget it, sister! I ain't leaving the kid alone!"

The woman raised both arms and the two ghosts began to disappear slowly. As they faded away, Zack heard Mad Dog Murphy's voice echoing off the walls in some kind of tunnel: "I'll be back, kid! You'll see! I'm comin' back to get you, Zack Jennings!"

All of a sudden, Zack didn't feel so hungry. How did this ghost know his name? None of the others ever did.

He decided maybe he'd skip breakfast, go back to the room, pack his suitcase.

"Are you okay?" asked the girl who had been staring at him.

"Yeah."

Now her mother was staring at him, too. "Are you sure?" the mother asked. "You look like you just saw a ghost."